MURDER, MAISEY, & OOPSI-DAISIES

An Annie Graceland Cozy Mystery

PAMELA SUE DUMOND
PAMELA DUMOND

Stay in the loop! Sign up for Pam's Newsletter .

COZY MYSTERIES

ANNIE GRACELAND COZY MYSTERIES - *Stand Alones*

Murder, Maisey, & Oopsi-Daisies
Murder, Screams, & Drama Queens — Coming soon
Cupcakes, Signs, & Valentines: A Novella
Cupcakes, Pies, & Hometown Guys
Cupcakes, Sales, & Cocktails
Cupcakes, Diaries, & Rotten Inquiries
Cupcakes, Paws, & Bad Santa Claus
Cupcakes, Bats, & Scaredy Cats
Cupcakes, Bars, & Rock Stars
Cupcakes, Spies, & Despicable Guys
Cupcakes, Lies, & Dead Guys

***Annie Graceland's* CHEESEHEAD MYSTERIES** -
Stand Alones

The Case of the Sugar Plum Shenanigans
The Case of the Candy King's Catastrophe - Coming soon

VON PUMPERNICKLE COZY MYSTERIES -
Stand Alones
Goldmitten
Dr. StrangeDove — Coming soon

THRILLERS

***MORTAL BELOVED TIME TRAVEL* Thrillers**

The Messenger #1
The Assassin #2
The Seeker #3
The Believer #4: Jack & Clara — *STAND ALONE*

***21st CENTURY COURTESAN* Psychological Thrillers** - *Series*

THE PLAYER #1

THE MOVIE STAR #2
THE BELOVED #3
THE HUSBAND #4
THE DEVOTED FAN #5

'SWEETER' ROMANCE

ROYALLY WED ROM-COM - *Series*

Part-time Princess #1 — Optioned for Film/TV.
Royally Wed #2
Part-time Poser #3
Royally Knocked Up #4

PLAYING SWEETER ROM-COM - *Stand Alones*

The Story of You and Me
Ms. Match Meets a Millionaire
The Stupidest Holiday of the Year - A Short Story
My Big Fake Mafia Wedding - Coming Soon

'HOT' ROMANCE

THE CROWN AFFAIR - *Series*

The Prince's Playbook #1

His Majesty's Measure #2
The American Princess #3
The Duchess's Decision #4

&

PLAYING DIRTY ROM-COM - *Stand Alones*

The Client
The Matchmaker
The Bodyguard

&

Stay in the loop! Sign up for <u>Pam's Newsletter</u> !

COPYRIGHT

Copyright © 2022 by Pamela DuMond

All rights reserved.

"Murder, Maisey, & Oopsi-Daisies" is an original work of fiction.

All names, characters, places, and incidents are the product of the author's imagination and/or are used fictitiously. Any resemblance to actual events, locales, or persons, living or dead, is coincidental.

No part of this book may be used or reproduced by any means, graphic, electronic, or mechanical, including photocopying, recording, taping, or by any other means, without written permission of the author, except in the use of brief quotations used in articles or reviews.

Neither are persons allowed to re-write or repurpose this book. That makes it a **derivative** book which is also **a violation of copyright law.**

You can contact the author via her website for permission to reference this book at www.pameladumond.com .

Stock Photos

Cover Copyright by Glammypammy

Pamela DuMond Media

DESCRIPTION

USA Today Best author featured on "ABC 20/20" brings you another hilarious Annie Graceland mystery!

Annie Graceland: Cheesehead. Unwed. Hi-LAR-ious baker who speaks to 'The Dead!'

I'm interviewing with nice-guy, Venice Beach tech million-aire Mason Callaway to cater the desserts at his birthday bash. His name can open doors and I really want this gig.

So, I go for it. I pop on Instagram and research his foodie posts. I spend hours concocting confections for him to taste. I'm waiting at a microbrewery to meet up with him when a Boho-styled brunette clutching a beer trips on her six-inch platforms.

She hurtles through the air and douses me in pale ale, before catching herself on top of the pastry box. My samples are smashed. Chocolate is everywhere.

"Oopsi-daisies," she says. "I'm Maisey."

Maisey is Mason's ex-GF who's been semi-stalking him. He filed a temporary restraining order. She doesn't care. I still get the birthday bash catering gig.

What could possibly go wrong?

🙰

"Publishers Weekly calls Annie Graceland stories **"… blithe and funny contemporary cozy mystery…"**

Murder, Maisey, & Oopsi-Daisies contains a recipe and is also available in Print.

Annie Graceland novels can be read as STAND ALONES!

🙰

Stay in the loop! Sign up for <u>Pam's Newsletter</u> .

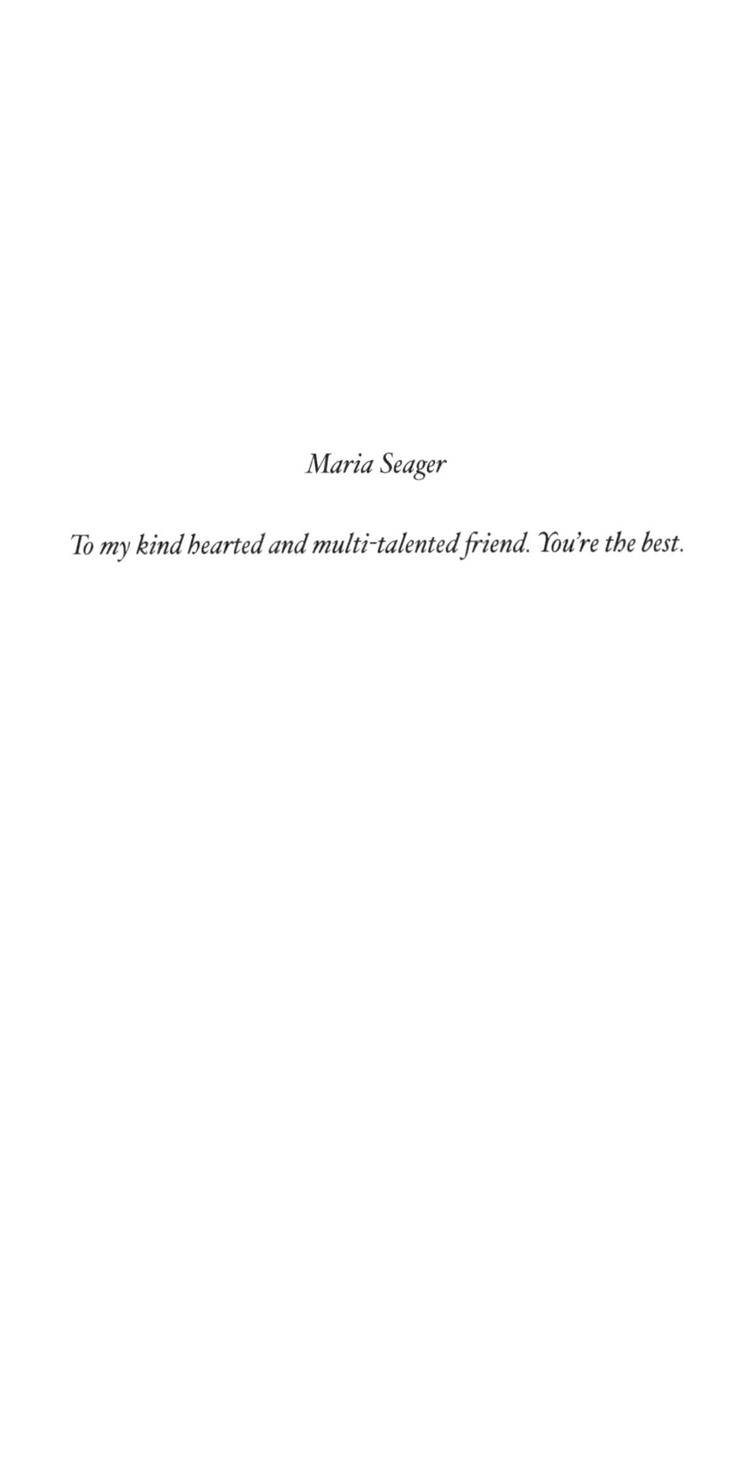

Maria Seager

To my kind hearted and multi-talented friend. You're the best.

❦   I   ❦

Chapter 1

A BIT of an EYESORE

❦

I pick up my beer at Moto Gear's long gleaming wooden bar and tip the young, tatted bartender generously. Moto Gear is a microbrewery that squats on a commercial street corner sandwiched between a florist and a barbershop in Venice Beach, California.

It used to be a motorcycle repair shop until the owners retired and moved to Arizona. The shop sat empty for years, became a bit of an eyesore, until someone saw past the graffiti and greasy floors, and recognized this space had great bones. They renovated the garage and turned it into a grungy but cool microbrewery, with a motorcycle theme.

Now I walk through the trendy brewery and head toward the outdoor patio. It's late February. Technically it's still winter, but it's also a sweater-weather kind of day. The walls are lined with glossy photos of motorcycles and attractive people riding them. Biker gear is for sale in metal cubicles lining dark wood walls. Rock 'n' roll music plays through invisible speakers in the background.

I carry a beer in one hand and an Annie Graceland's Killer Confections bag, carefully packed with freshly baked desserts, in the other. I slip outside a door onto the terrace. Wind, with a hint of a chill, rustles palm tree fronds. Sun shines but there's a nip in the air.

It's three in the afternoon, post-lunch, but pre-after-work crowd. Not too busy. I make my way to a two-top table next to a fence covered in white and pink trailing roses. I place my Killer Confections bag carefully on the table. The paper bag is crisp and white, adorned with the super cute logo that I'd recently designed: a big, fat cupcake with a serrated knife jutting out from it.

I take a seat and sip from the pale ale. Beer isn't usually my thing, but it seemed kind of stupid to order anything else at a microbrewery. The ale has a "hoppy taste," is a little citrusy, and a hint of a tang lingers on my tongue. It's relaxing. I'm normally a pile of nerves before a meeting this important. Having one beer won't kill me.

I'd gotten a text when I walked into Moto that my potential new client was running a few minutes late. I decided to use this extra time to practice my pitch in my head, center myself, and be at my very best when I met Mason Callaway, yes—*the* Mason Callaway, a relatively new mega-millionaire on the Venice Beach block.

A few years back, Mason was your run-of-the-mill dot-com guy. Then the real estate gods smiled down upon him. He bought a smattering of properties in Venice at just the right time. Within five years, real estate prices doubled, my sleepy little neighborhood woke up, and Mason Meier had spun sand into gold.

He was turning fifty in less than a week and was throwing himself an upscale casual birthday bash. He wanted to feature local caterers and bakers because supporting the neighborhood was part of Mason's brand. He had his entire party planned until his dessert person bailed, some kind of family emergency. His assistant contacted local shopkeepers for a replacement. My pal Sadie, who owned the cutest plant shop in all of Venice, mentioned me.

When I got Mason's text, I nearly fell off my chair. I picked my jaw up off the floor and promptly texted him back. *Yes,* I personally made all my own baked goods. *Yes,* I used only the best ingredients. And, yes, you'd better believe I wanted this job.

Catering the desserts for Mason Callaway's event would expose me to a higher class of clientele. Folks who wouldn't think twice about shelling out a decent chunk of change to buy desserts that were made from scratch and baked with love—not cheap, off-the-shelf junk.

His party was this Friday—did I have the time slot available?

Yikes—short notice. I'd already promised my part-time boss, Mort Feinberg, of Feinberg's Famous Deli, that I'd bake three hundred bar mitzvah cupcakes for his great-grandson's epic celebration. But I was a terrific multi-tasker. Why couldn't I do both?

I texted him back immediately.

Annie: Yes, I can absolutely make that work.

My nerves did the cha-cha in my stomach.

Mason: Great. Do you mind if we meet first? I'd love to sample a few of your pastries.

Annie: Perfect.

And so, while I worked on those bar mitzvah cupcakes, I also researched. I stalked Mason on social media, taking note of anything he posted about food. He sported a non-fussy haircut and wore casual clothes that made him look like the man who had invested wisely was still the down-to-earth boy next door. I got the feeling that he appreciated the finer things in life but didn't want to come across as arrogant or entitled.

I tried to figure out what he liked from the kinds of restaurants he frequented. Was he into Italian trattorias? Upscale vegan joints? Old-school steakhouses?

But Mason wasn't much of a social media poster. Once in a while he'd be tagged in a group shot at an eatery, but he was just as likely to be photographed eating a hot dog at a baseball game or sipping a lemonade watching a skateboarding competition.

I percolated on which desserts might work best for his party. I spent the next afternoon baking a garden variety of samples and taste-tested the lot. I selected the yummiest—placing fat cupcakes, juicy tarts, and boozy mini-cheesecakes into a pastry box. I slipped that inside the bag emblazoned with my logo.

Now I sit on Moto Gear's outdoor patio, sipping my pale ale, enjoying what's left of the afternoon sun and give myself a silent pep talk.

"Annie Graceland," my imaginary pep-talk coach, who I call "Sister Cecelia Videlia" says in my head, *"You could have slacked off. You could have bought someone else's cakes for the bar mitzvah and passed them off as your own. Seriously, Mort Feinberg is as old as Methuselah. I don't think he would have known."*

"But that would be dishonest and a rotten thing to do," I silently say.

"You worked hard and did your homework, my child."

"Thanks. You know me. I'm a hardworking, homework kind of girl."

The *real* Sister Cecelia Videlia was a former nun as well as my Sunday school teacher when I was in the fourth grade. I picked her to be the face of my *imaginary* pep-talk coach, not only because she gave great advice, knew how to turn lemons into lemonade, but also because she'd been struck by lightning three times and lived to talk about it.

Sister Cecelia knew about miracles. After the first lightning strike, Sister Cecelia's hair took on a life of its own. It stuck out at odd angles, making her look like Big Bird. She didn't sit around and complain about it. She invented an organic hair moisturizing mask and made a pretty penny.

After the second lightning strike, Sister Cecelia discovered she could converse with dead celebrities. Back in the third grade, she regaled us kids with stories about conversations she had with Elvis, First Lady Eleanor Roosevelt, and, of course, Pierre Picaud—the real-life vengeful French shoemaker who was the inspiration for *The Count of Monte Cristo*: the book, not the sandwich.

After the third lightning strike, she got an afternoon TV talk show called *Sister Cecelia Talks to Dead Celebs*, which ran for about five years. I've never had a TV show, and I've never been struck by lightning, but we had enough in common.

"*I give you an A-plus on your prep skills,*" imaginary Sister Cecelia says. "*Not only did you research your potential client, you baked a terrific variety of delicious desserts.*"

"*Thank you,*" I reply, somewhat smug.

"*You're welcome,*" she says. "*Now take the rest of this down-time to say prayers or meditate, if you wish, but honestly? I think you've got this.*"

"*Will do.*"

"*Gotta go, kiddo. Off to hit a few balls before a storm pops up. I don't play sports during thunderstorms anymore. I can only do the lightning -strike thing so many times. Too many surprises can kill a girl.*"

"*I hear you.*" I, too, hate unexpected surprises. I like being prepared.

Now I lean back in my chair and stretch my legs. Sister Cecelia is right; this job interview is going to go great. This interview is going to be a total cakewalk.

"Oopsi daisies," a woman says.

I glance up.

A woman hurtles through the air, heading in my direction, a panicked look on her face. Her outstretched hand white-knuckles a server's tray, but that doesn't stop the large pitcher of beer from tipping off it as time.. slows... down.

I throw up a hand in front of my face, which does not help one iota. A second later, I'm drenched in sticky beer. The acrylic pitcher bounces off my forearm, smacks the table, and clatters onto the ground. I have beer shirt. Beer hair. Beer down there. There isn't just a little tang inside my mouth—there's a little tang everywhere.

My dreams of catering Mason Callaway's party dive like panicked lemmings off a cliff. But, miraculously, my Annie Graceland's Killer Confections bag sits on the table with only a small splotch of beer on it. I breathe a sigh of relief. The desserts are safe.

When the Oopsi Daisies woman crashes into me. She lands half on my lap and half on the table. The tray goes flying and she catches herself on top of my sampler container with an "Oof!" and I cringe.

"Hey, Maisey. You okay?" a man asks. "You need help?"

"Nope." the woman replies, gritting her teeth. "I'm fine."

But my desserts aren't. Chocolate oozes out of a gash in the white pastry bag and my heart sinks. I stretch an arm out for it, but I'm pinned by the woman still flailing on top of me. "Can I help you? Are you all right?" I ask.

"Yes. No," she says, crawls off and stands up. She shakes her foot, then places weight on it. "I think so."

"Good," I say and grab my bag, desperately hoping that all the desserts aren't ruined. Maybe I can salvage some. Maybe like Sister Cecelia, I can make lemonade. I pull out the cupcake. It's squished. Chocolate icing and multi-colored sprinkles ooze between my fingers.

"I'm so sorry," she says. "I didn't mean to trip and fall. You have no idea how hard I've been working on this. Are you, alright?"

"Nothing that a little soap and water won't fix," I said. "What do you mean you've been working so hard on this?"

"My name's Maisey Miller," she says and bites her lip. "And I have a problem."

"Annie Graceland," I say. "Tell me more."

"I'm a bit of an airhead and sometimes a klutz. If

there's something to trip over – I stumble over it. If there's a kitchen towel that's lying too close to a stovetop? I'm the one who sets it on fire. I'm currently enrolled in a program designed to teach me how to be more present, which I'm assured, will make me less klutzy."

It's nice she blurted out her flaws up front, but I'm not willing to tell her my own deep dark secrets. Not going to share that I talk to murdered dead people. Definitely not going to confide that murdered dead people talk back to me, nagging me to find their killers. "They have programs to help you be less of a klutz?"

"They have programs for everything these days," Maisey says.

"You're right." I picture Sister Cecelia and silently ask. *"Do they have programs for ghost whisperers who don't want to be ghost whisperers anymore?"*

"Yes. It's called exorcism. I'm on the ninth hole. Don't interrupt my Zen."

"In my defense," Maisey says. "I come from a long line of clumsy people. It runs in the blood."

"I hope you didn't trip over me," I say, checking the other desserts. The boozy cheesecakes and the tarts survived the accident with barely a nick. I cross myself because I suspect it's a little Sister Cecelia miracle.

"I think I tripped over the guy seated at the table behind you." Maisey tips her head in his direction. "I know him. He works with my old boyfriend."

I swivel and look. "The metro guy with too much facial hair?"

She nods. "He jutted his knee into the aisle out of nowhere. Man-spreading."

Oh, that guy's man-spreading all right. He's also not all

that contrite, laughing about something with his friend while a bruise blossoms on Maisey's arm and I'm doused in beer.

"You have a smudge of chocolate frosting on your forehead," she says. "But that's okay. It's Ash Wednesday."

"Thanks." Probably from when I crossed myself. I pick up the tray and napkins that lie scattered on the ground. I dab at my face, my shirt. "Do you waitress here?"

"No," she shakes her head. "I'm meeting a writer friend for a drink and gossip. I'm a writer too. We live in our heads a lot, you know, working on stories. I think this might contribute to my problem. By the way, you have chocolate frosting with sprinkles on your chest."

"Huh." I dab at them.

"What brings you here to Moto Gear on this lovely afternoon?" she asks.

"An interview. I'm a baker. I'm meeting a guy who's interested in hiring me to cater the desserts for his party."

"Fun," she says, then eyes my squashed pastry bag with chocolate oozing out. "Oh no. These were your samples. I ruined them, didn't I?"

"Only the cupcake."

"I'll make it up to you. I promise."

A tall man wearing dark sunglasses approaches. He has light brown hair and shoulders like a linebacker. "Annie Graceland?"

"Yes?"

"Pete Jones."

"Hey, Pete," Maisey says, smiling up at him.

"I can't talk with you, Maisey. Remember?" He frowns. "Ms. Graceland, can I have a moment?"

My gaze ping-pongs between the two of them. "Sure.

But I might have to cut it short. I have an appointment. He's running a little late."

"Oh my God." Maisey's hand flies to her chest. "You're meeting Mason Callaway, aren't you?"

"Yes." I nod.

"Mason sent me in his place," Pete says. "Something's come up. He was hoping you'd be willing to meet him at his beach house. I can drive you there."

"The Marina del Rey beach house?" Maisey asks. "Or the Malibu house? I love both. Can I tag along?"

"No," Pete says. "The temporary restraining order is still in effect."

"Aha," I say, eyeing Maisey in a new light.

"That judge didn't know what she was doing," she says.

"Ready to meet Mason?" Pete asks. "I know he's excited to meet you."

"Yes," Maisey says.

"Not you," Pete says.

"I'm not exactly meet-able," I say, plucking at my soggy clothes.

He gives me the once-over. "You're soaked in pale ale, covered in chocolate and icing with sprinkles on top. What more could a guy want?"

"I'm interviewing for the job as the dessert caterer. Not the actual dessert."

"Maisey." A woman waves. She walks through Moto Gear's back door, onto the patio, and heads in our direction.

She looks familiar, and then I realize why. She is Clarissa Pinkowski, the trust-fund heiress who throws all the weirdly themed parties. I used to cater for her until she stiffed me, and claimed everything that went wrong with her zoo-themed party was my fault. It was not my fault that Mikey the marmoset grabbed a cupcake from my dessert stand and threw it at her guest of honor.

"You're still friends with Clarissa?" Pete asks.

"What do you care," Maisey says. "You're not talking to me."

"Right," he says. "Of course. Anything you say, Duchess. Ready to go, Ms. Graceland?"

"Yes. Nice to meet you, Maisey." I walk toward the patio door before Clarissa reaches our table. She probably won't remember me as I'm so many rungs below her on the social ladder. But you never know.

"Darling." Clarissa reaches Maisey and they air-kiss. "Sorry I'm late. Hey, is that Pete?"

"Yes," Maisey says. "But he's not talking to me."

"Ugh. Stuffy Pete. He's always been a little 'Daddy' with you," she says.

I can't get out of Moto Gear fast enough.

In the parking lot, Pete and I make our way toward a dark SUV. I smell beer, wonder if I have toothpaste in my purse, and then realize toothpaste isn't going to do the trick. "Can we make a pit stop? My place? Super quick?"

"Yes," he says.

"Annie," Maisey says.

I turn and see her holding the smooshed cupcake in one outstretched hand. "You almost forgot this."

"Right," I say, walk a few steps and take it from her. "Thanks."

Pete backs the SUV out of the parking space and pulls next to me. He rolls down the window and gives me a look.

"I get a good feeling, Annie," Maisey says. "I think you're going to nail this job interview. I'll be in touch."

"Sounds great," I say and get in the car. But the truth of the matter? I don't think I care if I ever see Maisey Miller again.

❦ 2 ❦

Chapter 2

THIS ZONKERS IDEA

❦

Pete waits outside my apartment in the SUV and blasts 1990s songs.

I duck inside my one-bedroom modest abode and take the quickest shower in the world. I throw on decent jeans and a clean, long-sleeved cashmere shirt. I run a comb through my hair. I grab a fresh pastry bag from the kitchen, and for that matter, a non-squished chocolate cupcake. I'm out the door in ten minutes flat.

"Quickest turnaround ever." Pete opens the back door and I hop inside his car. He starts the engine and pulls away from the curb.

"Are we headed to the house in the Marina or the one in Malibu?"

"Marina," he says. "But Mason's party's going to be at his Malibu house."

"He has two houses?" I ask.

"The Marina Del Rey place is his city house. The Malibu place is his get-away pad."

"Got it," I say. "Can I ask you something?"

"Sure."

"Why is there a temporary restraining order against Maisey?"

"I'm not supposed to talk about that," Pete says, turning a corner as we make our way down a cut-through street, lined with three-story apartment buildings and a few eateries.

"Okay."

"I'm not even supposed to talk to *her.* We used to hang out, you know. Before the *thing.*"

"The thing?" I ask.

"I feel horrible about the thing," Pete says, making a left at the light onto a street in the Marina. We wind past tall, glassy apartment buildings that rent for about twice what I'm paying for my hovel because they are bright and shiny and have swimming pools.

"I don't blame you," I say, sorely tempted to ask him what the thing is.

The road dead ends into a lane alongside a pretty water channel dotted with boats traveling between the Marina's docks and the Santa Monica Bay.

"Maisey's not a bad girl. She's funny, creative, pretty. A little wacky, if you know what I mean."

"Not really."

"She's a dreamer, a believer in new age philosophy, and phenomena. She even wrote a book about it."

"Really?"

"The Urban Witch," he says. "Sometimes I think she lives in a fantasy world. Which was fine, until she got this zonkers idea that she and Mason were meant to be."

"Meant to be?"

"Spiritually connected."

"Aha," I say. "Tell me more?"

"Can't." His aviator sunglasses reflect the setting sun in the rearview mirror.

"Okay."

"It didn't help that Mason flew her to Aspen and put her up at his chalet so she could work on her second book. He thought the environment might be peaceful Nurturing. Calm her down."

"Was it?"

"Maybe," he says, pulling down a street and making a left into the driveway of a three-story, minimalist, modern-styled house. "Until he started sleeping with her." He parks in the immaculate driveway, the garage door open. Inside is a high-end Land Rover and a sleek Porsche.

"Uh-oh."

Pete hops out of the driver's seat and opens my door. "Her new book was half-done. They flew back from Aspen. Mason announced he wanted to see other people. That didn't go over well."

"Most women who are flown to Aspen and slept with do not like to be put on the side thereafter," I say, stepping out of the car. "Women are not a layaway plan."

"Ha," he says. "You're funny."

"I'm serious." We make our way through the garage, pass a few dirt bikes, a gleaming black-and-red Harley Davidson motorcycle. Pete pops open a door into the house. He gestures for me to go first. I hear the sound of the garage door closing.

We enter the laundry room. A large, sleek cherry-red washer-and-dryer set are humming. Overhead racks hold folded towels, crates of grocery staples. A tall, shiny stainless-steel freezer rests in the corner. "I've never seen a washer this pretty," I say, running a hand over it.

"Mason likes pretty things," Pete says, moving past me.

I follow him into the kitchen and look around, feeling a like I've landed in a Mr. Tidy commercial. This room is pristine, modern. There are white wood floors and white cabinetry with clean lines and elegant pulls. Black-and-white marble countertops. A round three-tiered rack of fruit sits in one corner, the row of apples so red, I half wonder if my eyes are bleeding. "There's not a dishrag out of place."

"Just the way Mason likes it," Pete says, moving into the adjoining living room. New Age music plays through invisible speakers. Floor-to-ceiling windows look out over a deck and a back yard that leads to Silicon Beach.

There's a scattering of volleyball courts and a walkway along the multimillion-dollar houses that line up along the sand. The sun is a ball of fire sinking over the Pacific Ocean. A few people stroll close to the waves as they hit the sand. There's a couple of joggers. Dogs gleefully frolic in and out of the water. A scattering of sailboats putter toward the channel on their way back to the docks.

"Take a seat," Pete says. "Can I get you anything?"

"I'm good for now, thanks."

The living room has a vaulted ceiling. The space features two modern, lean leather couches. A rectangular metal coffee table rests between them. A square accent chair is placed on an angle adjacent to the marble fireplace. If chairs could talk, this one would say, "I'm just here for decoration. Please don't sit on me." Two flat-screen TVs are mounted high on walls. An abstract oil painting is situated over a large copper-topped water wall trickling onto dark stones, tall ficus plants situated on either side.

"What do you think about the place?" Pete asks.

"Wouldn't this be a nice view to come home to every day? It's very…" I search for the word. "Cold" doesn't sound right. "Sterile" isn't the kindest word.

"Zen," Pete says. "Another reason why I could never picture Maisey and Mason together. Maisey's the opposite of Zen. She's like warm apple pie with a dash of cinnamon, and a pinch of pixie dust. Mason's more angles and algorithms."

I shrug. "Who knows why people connect." Speaking of connecting, maybe I should have texted my friends to tell them I was headed here—wherever here is. Yes, I'm in the Marina, but I don't have the actual address. The only person who knows I accepted a ride from Pete is Maisey. Not only is Maisey a ditz, she's been hit with a temporary restraining order, which puts her on my suspicious list.

Who else is on my suspicious list, you might ask? Politicians. Braggarts. People who tell you everything's okay at the same time they're shaking their head. And people with restraining orders.

I glance around. Am I even *in* Mason Callaway's house? I'm hanging out in a multimillion-dollar beachfront mansion with a tall, muscular man I don't know. I'm suddenly riddled with guilt because I just violated one of my mother's big "No-nos."

I accepted a ride from a stranger.

When I was a kid Mom told me a million times to *never* accept rides from strangers. I followed her rule religiously up until a half hour ago when I agreed to accept a ride from Pete, a complete stranger.

To make matters worse, I haven't even spotted Mason Callaway since I landed in this posh place. Nor have I received a follow-up message to his "I'm going to be a little late." text from over an hour ago. I clutch my white pastry bag in my sweaty palm a little tighter. Am I getting myself into some kind of trouble?

"Other than not following your mother's practical advice?" Sister Cecelia, my imaginary pep-talk coach, asks silently. *"No."*

"Phew," I silently say.

"Besides, what's going to happen? You're too old to be trafficked," she says.

"And, my family's too middle class for anyone to kidnap me and want a ransom," I say. *"What should I do? Sneak back through the kitchen? Run out the garage door?"*

"No. The big guy closed it."

"Aha," I say. *"Grab my phone from my purse and conk him over the head?"*

"No," Sister Cecelia says. *"Always lead with the practical solutions. Just like I taught you kids in Sunday school."*

"What's the practical solution?"

"Ask him where Mason is."

I turn to Pete who's seated at a table checking his messages. "Where's Mason?"

"Here." Mason Callaway walks into the living room, slipping his phone into his pocket. I inhale. In person, he looks just like his online pictures: thick chestnut hair, six feet tall. He's built lean but not thin. He's dressed in a long-sleeved, fitted gray T-shirt, black jeans, and flip-flops. "You must be Annie Graceland. Thanks for meeting me." He extends a hand.

"Nice to meet you too." We shake.

"Can I get you anything to drink?" Pete asks, standing up.

"Seltzer water for me. Annie?" Mason asks.

"Make that two. Thanks."

"Got it," Pete says and disappears into the kitchen.

"Sorry I was late for our meeting," Mason says, opening the door to his deck.

"Apology accepted." I follow him outside.

"I'm negotiating this deal for a clothing brand with a guy that makes me a little crazy. You probably know how temperamental some of these creative types can be."

"Yes." The sun is halfway down the waterline, the sky a blend of purples, and crimsons, and blues and I shiver from the crisp ocean air.

"Chilly?" Mason asks.

"Yes," I say, taking a seat. I place my pastry bag on the coffee table. The deck is white-washed wooden planks, the furniture geometric but looks comfier than the living room pieces. A closed umbrella stands next to a stainless steel gleaming BBQ.

"The temperature at the beach drops quickly when the sun goes down," he says. He leans toward a heat lamp and turns up the dial. The lamp hums and the air quickly grows warm.

Pete steps onto the deck and places two bottles of Pellegrino and glasses on the table. "Anything else?"

"Thanks. We're good," Mason says.

"Do you want me to stay and drive Ms. Graceland home?"

"Go. You're off the clock."

Pete salutes and leaves.

Mason takes a seat across from me. "Are these your samples?"

"Yes." I smile. "Help yourself."

He pulls out the napkins I packed first, next the cupcake, and sinks his teeth into it. I think his eyes roll back in his head. "Wow."

"Double dark," I say. "I don't scrimp on the chocolate."

He reaches inside the bag, pulls out the wedge of cheesecake, and takes a bite.

"Kahlua?" he asks.

"And bourbon. I also don't scrimp on the booze."

"I no longer feel bad that the other baker left me at the last minute." He takes another bite. There's a smudge of cream cheese on his lower lip. "My party's this Friday. It's last minute, but if you want the job, you're hired."

"For real?"

His phone pings.

"For real," he says, downing his water. He stands and checks his text.

I get why Maisey was attracted to him. I'm in love with Detective Raphael Campillio, but Mason's a tall, cool glass of water on a warm day.

"Apologies," he says. "I've got to change clothes and blow out of here. Meeting that crazy designer for a sit-down. You live in Venice, right?"

"Yes."

"Want me to drop you on the way?"

"That would be great," I say and stand.

"Give me ten minutes. I'll meet you in the kitchen," he says, crosses the living room. He holds his phone close to his face as he jogs up the stairs, taking them two at a time. "Talk to me."

❧

TEN MINUTES. Ho hum.

What can an overly curious baker with a pinch of psychic ability do with ten minutes inside a beachfront mansion owned by a multimillionaire?

If one were prudent, one would take a seat on a barstool next to the kitchen counter and wait patiently. I do that for a bit, scroll through my phone, check social media, but quickly grow bored.

I explore the kitchen. The shiny stainless-steel fridge sports only two magnets. One—a business card for Johnny's Pizzeria. Two—a photo of Mason and a not completely unfortunate looking honey blonde woman. His arm is wrapped around her. They're holding skis and standing on a snow-covered slope that looks remarkably like Aspen. I can't help but wonder how quickly he moved on to the next girl after Maisey.

"You've got ants in your pants," Sister Cecelia says. *"Take a seat."*

"Right." I sit back on the barstool and stare at the perfectly shaped, shiny red apples displayed on a fruit stand. They look like art. I am tempted to eat one.

"Not a good idea," Sister Cecelia says.

"Who's going to notice?" I ask.

"Whoever polished them and lined them all up at exactly the same angle to look magazine-cover perfect," Sister Cecelia says.

"Right. What if I explored the house for a bit? Only the first floor."

"Meh," Sister Cecelia says.

My phone pings.

Julia: Where are you?

Julia: You promised to help me look at stock photos tonight for my new website. I showed up with a pizza and you aren't home. I ordered extra pepperoni, just the way you like it.

I text back.

Annie: I'm sorry. I completely forgot.

Annie: Did you let yourself in?

Julia: Of course.

I leave the kitchen and walk down a hallway, phone still in hand.

Annie: I had that job interview with Mason Callaway. I lost track of time when our meeting was delayed.

Julia: Ohhh... Mason Callaway. He's hot for a tech-guy millionaire.

Annie: I know.

Julia: I forgive you.

Julia: I haven't eaten all the pizza yet.

Julia: Come home and tell me all about him.

I spy a closed door. Something about it feels intriguing. I check my watch. Mason said to give him ten minutes. Would it hurt to take a peek? I have plenty of time.

Annie: Will do. Keep looking at stock photos. Mark the ones you like.

Julia: I'm already doing that. Grady's on his way but you've got a better eye. When are you headed home?

I wiggle the knob.

Annie: Mason's dropping me off in a few.

Julia: Ooh, first name basis. Not fair. You have a boyfriend.

Annie: I know.

Julia: Is Mason dating material?

Annie: Yes, except I'm pretty sure he has a girlfriend.

The door opens. I walk inside. The room smells like eucalyptus. A universal fitness machine is in the center. Lined up against one wall is a rack of exercise equipment. Gym balls. Dumbbells in ascending weight order are neatly stacked next to it. A large basket holds exercise tubing and bands. I pick up a ten-pound dumbbell and do a few bicep curls.

"*Yeah, Arnold Schwarzenegger, you still have it,*" Sister Cecelia says. "*Go back to the kitchen. Stop touching things.*"

"*Okay,*" I say, ignore her, and walk farther into the room. French doors lead to a hot tub on a small side patio. My phone pings again.

> **Julia:** *Hey - I forgot to ask. Did you get the job?*

Annie: *Yes.*

> **Julia:** *Yay! See you in a bit.*

I love hot tubs. I love anything that smells fresh and clean like eucalyptus. I look at my watch. I've got a few more minutes until Mason returns. I'm tempted to strip off my clothes and jump in that tub but that would be stupid. No one in their right mind would do something like that.

When a drenched head pops out of the water. "Hey."

"Ahhhh!" I scream.

❧ 3 ☙

Chapter 3

A HUMBLE BAKER

❧

I slap a hand over my mouth.

"Shh." The woman places a finger to her lips, wet hair plastered on her face.

"Maisey?"

"It's not Mother Theresa." She pulls herself out of the tub, naked.

Clearly, she's not Mother Theresa. I avert my eyes, but the patio's small. I stare upward, straight into the lens of a security camera. *Crap.* Maybe I should have stayed in the kitchen. "What are you doing here?"

"I miss this house." She walks to a bench, reaches for a towel, and dries herself off. She wraps it around her. "Especially the hot tub. The jets are strong. I took quite the

25

tumble back there at Moto Gear when I tripped over the man-spreader."

"Aren't you under a restraining order?" I ask. "Aren't you supposed to be a certain number of yards away from Mason and his property?"

"Oh that." She waves a hand in the air. "That wasn't Mason's idea. One of his people talked him into it."

Yes, but what did Maisey do to provoke that?

"Besides, no one will ever know I'm here," she says. "I'll get dressed and slip out the side gate."

I glance up. "It's locked."

"Thank God, I still have a spare key," she says. "How did you think I got in?"

"I don't know. What if they catch you on surveillance video?"

"Then the security guys will enjoy the view," she says. "Congrats on getting the baking gig. In spite of the murky energy clouding your aura, I had a feeling you would."

"Annie," Mason calls from the kitchen. "We need to get going."

"Be right there," I holler, then turn back to her. "How did you know I got the baking gig?"

"I overheard Mason tell you." Maisey shrugs on her clothes. "Jeez, it's not like I'm psychic."

"You were outside? On the deck?"

"Of course not, silly," she says. "I was in the living room."

In the living room? That space was minimalist. Pristine. My stomach flip-flops. "I never saw you."

"How could you see me? I was hiding behind the ficus." She wriggles her key in the lock. "The one next to the water wall. What a monstrosity that thing is, eh? I told

Mason not to buy it. I told him an overpriced trickling fountain wouldn't make his anxiety better. But God forbid he ever listened to me. Everybody in the world wants something from Mason Callaway except for me. I just loved him for who he was: quirks and all."

For a moment, she no longer looks completely batshit. She looks young, a little lost, and reminds me of my cousin, Izzy who lives in Wisconsin. My irritation hits the brakes while my heart goes out to her. "You know what they say about loving someone?"

"Better to have loved than never to have loved at all?" she asks.

"No."

"If you love someone, set them free?" she asks.

"No."

"Annie," Mason calls.

"Coming," I say and walk a few feet to the door.

"Love means never having to say you're sorry?"

"No." I shake my head. "Just... it's *okay* you loved him. I'm sorry it didn't work out. My friend says that every time you miss someone you love, to silently send them blessings. Do that over and over until one day, you won't miss them so much anymore."

"Blessings. Hmm. I like that," she says. "Again, apologies for the beer-spilling and squished-dessert debacles today. I will find a way to make it up to you."

"No worries," I say. "We're good."

"Ever have your aura cleansed? I can help you with that. I'm licensed as a certified aura cleanser."

"No." I turn back to her. "Please, Maisey." The words spill from my mouth. "Please be more careful, or you might get into serious trouble someday. Something you can't hide behind. Something a soak in the hot tub won't fix."

#

My best friends sprawl on opposite sides of my couch absorbed in their electronic devices. The three of us share a pepperoni pizza, the grease-stained Johnny's Pizza box rests on the coffee table between us.

Grady, a thirty-something geeky guy, types on his laptop balanced on his knees.

Julia, my BFF since high school, scrolls through her tablet, stops, and holds it out in my direction. "Do you like this one?" It's a stock image photo of a polished, professional thirty-something woman in a suit sitting at a desk in a modern, well-appointed office.

"What's the vibe you're going for?" Grady asks.

"Take charge, professional lawyer who can competently handle business contracts," I say.

"Exactly," Julia says and clicks on the screen. "I'm buying this picture. What happened after you found that weirdo woman in Mason's hot tub?"

"The most embarrassing words fell out of my mouth." I plop on the living room floor and aim the remote at the TV.

"What?" she asks.

"Please be more careful, or you might get into serious trouble someday." I sounded exactly like my mother. Shoot me now and put me out of my misery." Theodore Von Pumpernickle, my enormous mix-breed Himalayan cat, head butts my arm as I click through channels, searching for his favorite show.

"This momentous event happens to almost everyone," Grady says. "Don't beat yourself up. Saying those kinds of things is practically a rite of passage."

"I can't believe that chick showed up at the beach house, let herself in, and took a dip in his Jacuzzi," Julia says. "That takes some serious—"

"I can believe it," Grady says. "I've met Maisey Miller. She'll say anything. She'll do anything."

"How do you know her?" I ask, waving the remote closer to the flat screen as Theodore bats at the device.

"She hangs with creative types and trust fund babies," Grady says. "I've seen her at indie movie premieres, book signings, and she's always at the best parties. Speaking of, am I going to be your plus-one for Mason Callaway's birthday bash?"

"No," Julia says. "I am. You got to be her plus-one at the last party. The one on Mulholland Drive a few weeks ago."

"That was an Irish wake," Grady says.

"Which counts as a party," Julia says.

"A copious amount of scotch was drunk by persons over the age of eighty," Grady says. "I was trapped in the middle of an orthopedic disaster waiting to happen."

"I remember that gig," I say.

"When's Mason's party?" Julia asks.

"Friday," I say, finally finding the show my cat likes. Anderson Cooper pops on the screen, and Theodore stares at him, transfixed. "Remember, I'm not an invited guest. I'm a dessert caterer. Boy, I hope I can pull this off."

"Why couldn't you?" Grady asks.

"The crowd is upscale. I'm a humble baker."

"Au contraire," Grady says. "You're a *talented* baker who

lives in Venice and has been building a following for a few years now."

My doorbell rings.

"Is your boyfriend stopping by?" Julia asks.

"No. Raphael's working tonight." I haven't seen my handsome detective boyfriend in a few days. We talk every night, but we're overdue for more than face time. "Can you see who it is?"

"Sure." Grady gets up off the couch and walks toward the door.

"If it's the church people, tell them I've been saved. If it's the Little Brothers of the Poor, tell them I'm poor too."

He salutes.

"What does it matter if you're catering desserts for a cute millionaire's birthday party?" Julia asks. "Or refilling cupcake stands for a backyard BBQ?"

"Mason's party is kind of a backyard BBQ on steroids," I say. "I'm used to working average gigs for normal people."

"You don't need to put Mason Callaway on a pedestal," Grady says. "Reframe your vision of him."

"Impossible. He owns entire blocks of Venice real estate."

"Picture him naked," Grady says, opening the door. "Even millionaires look like everybody else when they're naked."

"You're right. They do," Maisey says, standing on four-inch platforms. She clutches a bottle of Champagne. "Yay! I'm here. Oh good, you have pizza. I'm hungry."

"Maisey?" Grady asks.

"Hey, I know you," she says. "Grady, right?"

"Yup."

She leans in and they air-kiss.

"What are you doing here?" I ask.

"I figured out a way to make up for today." She walks into my apartment.

"No, seriously, what are you doing here?" I ask. "How do you know where I live?"

"Not that difficult." She holds up her phone and taps it.

"Everything's online," Grady says.

Theodore stops watching Anderson Cooper and switches his blue-eyed gaze to Maisey.

"I brought you bubbly," she says, holding up the bottle. "The good stuff. Dom Perignon 2010."

"Yay," Julia says and extends her hand. "Nice to meet you. I'm Julia."

"I know," Maisey says as they shake.

"You know my name?"

"Of course. You were tagged in a photo on Annie's Instagram page. Something about a beauty pageant in Wisconsin."

"I remember that," Grady says.

"Do you have glasses?" Maisey twists the metal wire on the bottle to get to the cork.

"On it." I stand and walk into the kitchen. I grab a few flutes from the cabinet when I hear a *pop*.

"I thought the bubbly might be a nice surprise," Maisey says.

"Oh, it is," I say.

Julia enters the kitchen and leans in next to me. "Is Maisey a little crazy?"

"Yes." I run the glasses under the water and towel them dry.

"It's part of how I plan to make things up to you," Maisey says from the other room.

"Seriously, you don't need to make up for anything," I say.

"I grabbed the Dom Perignon from Mason's fridge before I left the place," she says. "Why go to the store when he's got a better selection?"

Julia twirls a finger next to her head. "Careful." She scoops up the glasses and walks back into the living room.

That's when I smell it. Something's burning. I sneeze. "Everything all right out there?"

"Maisey's burning sage," Grady says.

"I thought I'd sage the place before I cleansed your aura," she says.

"Kind of you." I enter the living room and see a trail of smoke. My cat scurries down the hallway, low to the ground, furtively looking for a place to hide. He paws at a closet door. It gaps open and he squeezes inside. "I'm not sure I want my aura cleansed."

Maisey circles my living room, waving the wand to and fro.

I sneeze again. "I think I'm allergic."

"You're probably just cleaning out old energy. It has to come out some way, you know. I sensed this cloud around you after we met. Dead things. People from the past. People demanding that you do things for them. Solve true crimes?" She looks at me and raises one eyebrow. "Are people demanding that you solve cold cases?"

Julia glares at me, eyes widening.

"Oh, who isn't addicted to true crime documentaries?" I ask, cheery.

"Sage is good for you." Maisey thrusts the smoking

wand a little higher, a little wider. "Clears out residual energy lingering from past relationships. Gets rid of energetic clutter. Banishes the ghosts from your life."

Wouldn't that be nice?

"Why don't we aura cleanse another night?" I ask. "Let's enjoy the bubbly you brought and chill for a bit. I've got a long day of baking ahead of me tomorrow."

"I'm almost done," Maisey says, ignoring me. "Just finishing this little section next to your front window. I sense dark energy here."

"Fine," I say and pour four glasses.

"Crap," Grady says.

"Oh no," Julia says.

The fire alarm on my ceiling screeches.

"Oopsi-daisies," Maisey says, grabbing my living room curtains and yanking on them. The drapes and the rod crash to the floor. She stomps on them with her four-inch platforms.

"Get back!" Grady says as another panel starts to smoke. He grabs Maisey's arm and pulls her away.

"Sorry," she says. "I'm so sorry!"

4

Chapter 4

HOUDINI

But the curtains would not be put out with a little foot stomping. When I couldn't find my portable fire extinguisher, Grady raced to my neighbors and pounded on their door. My neighbor couldn't find his extinguisher either and called the fire department.

Five minutes after I doused the drapes with Dom Perignon, uniformed firemen strode in through my open front door. So much for top-notch bubbly, pizza night, and au revoir to my pretty floral-print curtains.

The officer in charge informs me a paramedic is on the scene. He wants everyone to be checked for signs of smoke inhalation or the ability to think clearly. I tell him that the curtains were on fire for literally under a minute. I doubt any physical damage has been done to me or my friends, including Maisey, the world's biggest klutz. But in regards to the ability to think clearly? That's a lost cause.

"Humor me," he says.

"Okay. Examine my friends first. I need to find my cat."

Julia, Grady, and Maisey shuffle outside. Maisey looks a little dazed. Perhaps having the authorities show has shut her up or at least put the fear of God into her. Either would be nice, because clearly none of my warnings have made a dent.

I grab the cat carrier from the kitchen pantry. I walk down the hallway to the bedroom on the hunt for Theodore. I suspect he's still in the linen closet or perhaps he panicked during all of the hullabaloo when the curtains were torched. He might have skedaddled into my room and hid under the bed. But there's no way I am leaving my fur baby here with the front door wide open. That would be all the encouragement he needed to make a "grand escape."

He's pulled a "Houdini" a few times. I don't want him venturing outside and disappearing like he did that one Halloween. That's when my apartment manager, Anthony Spiggottini, all around *not* a nice guy and control freak, trespassed into my home and left the door ajar.

Theodore got out along with my neighbor's dog. It took me a few days to find the both of them, and the whole experience scared the crap out of me. Karma came quickly for Anthony: he was murdered that very night. No, I *didn't* do it. (To procure the juicy details, read the book: Cupcakes, Bats, & Scaredy Cats.)

Now I spot my sixteen-pound cat jammed in the back

of the hall closet behind a laundry basket. The only thing completely hidden is his face because hiding is not his strong suit.

I grab him under his fluffy armpits and he squeaks a few times, hoarse, like a frog. "Yeah, yeah," I say. "Tell it to the cat therapist." I stuff him in his cat carrier and wince when I pick it up because he is heavy.

"*How big is Theodore?*" Sister Cecelia asks.

"*I don't know. Last time we were at the vet, he weighed in at a little under sixteen pounds.*"

"*That's a lot of cat,*" she says.

"*Tell me about it.*" I make my way toward the front door and take in the mess: the soggy, torched living room curtains strewn on the wooden floors.

The sad, bare windows that look out on the walkway leading to my apartment. They practically scream, "Hey, strange people who might be walking by. Have nothing else better to do? Peek inside my place."

"*How many days before Mason Callaway's birthday party?*" Sister Cecelia asks.

"*I bake tomorrow. The party's Friday night. So – two?*" Cat carrier in hand, I exit my apartment and make my way toward the lights blinking from the paramedics' truck parked curbside. "*Any thoughts on what I should do about Maisey? I just met her today, but there's some weird kind of attachment happening.*"

"*How so?*" Sister Cecelia asks.

"*I can't get rid of her. Maybe I harmed her in a past life. Maybe it's karma.*"

"*Maybe it's 'crazy,'*" Sister Cecelia says. "*I am not touching that one. It is a rabbit hole I do not want to dive down.*"

"What kind of pep talk coach are you?" I ask, spotting my friends chatting with the paramedic at the back of the van.

"The kind you made up in your head," she says.

"Right," I say. *"Thanks for the reminder."*

"Anytime. See you soon, chickadee," she says—and poof! She's gone.

"Everyone okay?" I ask my friends.

"Yup," Grady says.

"Just a little smudgy," Julia says.

"I'm so sorry," Maisey says. "I'll make it up to you."

"Don't," I say.

"Your turn," the paramedic says and beckons.

"Seriously, *don't* make it up to me." I hoist Theodore's cage inside the back of the van and then climb inside. I take a seat. The paramedic wraps a blood pressure cuff around my arm, and it squeezes with a little whir. "It's not a big deal. Everything will be fine."

"What if I stopped by tomorrow and helped you get ready for the party?" Maisey asks.

"No," I say.

"Blood pressure's a little high," the paramedic says. "Let's take it again."

I grit my teeth as the cuff squeezes harder.

"Phew, I had so much fun but I'm exhausted," Grady says. "I'm going to call it a night. Maisey, why don't I chaperone you back to your place?"

"That's so sweet of you," she says.

"Thank you," I silently mouth to him.

"Who's your plus-one for the party?" he asks.

"You are…" I say. "You are my *assistant* at the party."

"But, but…" Julia says.

"I can live with that." Grady turns to Maisey. "Let's get

you home safe and sound, lady. Only the best for you." He hustles her down the block.

Maisey stops in her tracks, swivels, and stares at me like a kid leaving for her first day at kindergarten. "I had so much fun today, Annie. It was, like, the best day, ever. Thank you."

"You're... welcome?"

"Help me, sweet baby Jesus," Julia whispers.

"Let's go," Grady says.

Maisey turns and follows him.

"Might want to get your blood pressure checked again this week," the paramedic says to me. "Any other concerns?"

"Nope," I say.

"You're free to go."

"Thanks." I scramble out of the back of the van and grab Theodore's cat cage. He's been deathly quiet since he got here.

Julia and I walk back toward my place. "Big day," she says. "Mason Callaway hired you. Your house was set on fire."

"Just the drapes."

"How are you feeling? You survive Hurricane Maisey?"

"I think so," I say as we enter my place. "Stick around for a bit? Help me clean the front windows and hang temporary curtains?"

"Do you still have leftover pastry samples from your job interview?"

"Yes." I hand her a bottle of glass cleaner and a roll of paper towels.

"Can I be your second plus-one at his party?"

"Yes."

"Go get the pastries." She starts cleaning. "I'm in."

&.

A DAY AND CHANGE LATER, Julia, Grady, and I drive north on picturesque Pacific Coast Highway, headed toward Malibu. Stacks of Annie Graceland Killer Cupcakes pastry boxes are neatly piled in the back of my beater hatchback.

We pass wide Santa Monica beaches with their volley-ball courts. The sandy strips narrow after Topanga Canyon Drive as does the highway. Gentle twists and turns on the main thoroughfare follow midsized beachfront cottages on the left and roads that lead up into hills and canyons on the right.

Fifteen minutes later, we pause at the stoplight next to Cross Creek shopping mart in Malibu. The outdoor mall's usually filled with flip-flop and sweatshirt-attired customers as well as the occasional tourist who figured out they'll spot more "celebrities" here than anywhere in Hollywood.

"Can we stop for a tuna melt?" Julia asks.

"Malibu Pantry has the best tuna melts," Grady says.

"No," I say.

"But the sharp cheddar bites my tongue in a good way," Julia says. "And I'm hungry."

"I'm working." The light turns green and I accelerate. "Didn't you eat beforehand?"

"No," she says. "I was waiting for Mason's party."

"You can't eat at these kinds of parties until the very end." Grady says.

"Why not?"

"Because you're my assistant," I say. "You're a server, not an invited guest."

Julia's awfully dressed up for a catering gig. Her hair's immaculate. Her makeup expertly applied. She's wearing false eyelashes. I think she just got a manicure. I suspect she forgot she's not a guest.

"Assistants still need to eat," she says. "Will you be subjecting me to harsh working conditions?"

"We're catering a gig for a tech millionaire at his Malibu beach house," I say. "How harsh could it be?"

We motor past surfers riding waves in the ocean. A quarter mile up I make a left off of Pacific Coast Highway and turn onto a side road. It runs past the fire station, a pet hospital, and a yoga center.

We drive down a lane that that leads to Mason's Malibu beach house. I stop at the security gate for the private community and am issued a pass to keep on my dashboard for the party's duration. Mason's assistant, a woman named Katie, had sent instructions to pull into his driveway to unload the car. I do exactly that. We hop out and get to work.

"I'll find a cart." Julia follows a few uniformed caterers into a side yard.

Grady and I unpack the boxes of desserts.

"Be careful," I say.

"Calm down, mother," Grady says. "I think you have PTSD from two days ago."

"How is Maisey?" I ask. "You get her home safe and sound?"

"Funny you should ask," Grady says. "We were halfway to her place in Santa Monica when her phone pinged with text after text after text. I felt like Zuzu and her petals in *It's a Wonderful Life*.

"Every time a bell rings, an angel gets its wings," I say, quoting the movie line.

"Maisey told me to pull over at a coffee shop in Santa Monica. She thanked me for the ride and got out. I haven't heard from her since," Grady says.

Unwelcome shivers travel down my spine.

Julia rolls a cart in our direction, its wheels rattling on the driveway. "I scored."

"I hope Maisey's okay," I say.

"I'm sure she's fine," Grady says. "Her types usually are."

"What's her type?" I ask.

He swirls a finger next to his head.

"Right," I say.

The three of us get to work, unloading and stacking the boxes on the cart. A valet man sets up his stand on the sweep of the driveway, a dozen or so yards from the front entrance. A fire-engine-red Mercedes convertible purrs into the driveway.

"What now, Boss?" Julia asks, eating one of my freshly baked cannolis.

"Set up for the party," I say. "And stop pilfering the desserts."

"Didn't you hear my stomach growl?" she asks. "You don't want me passing out on the job."

"Right."

The Mercedes' driver, a woman wearing dark sunglasses with a thick scarf wrapped around her neck pulls up behind me, rolls to a stop.

The passenger door opens and a man steps out. It's the guy from the coffee shop. The one that Maisey tripped over. I remember she said he worked with her ex-boyfriend. "See you inside," he says to the woman in the sunglasses. "I need to catch Mason before the party gets going."

"Just go, David."

"I am. I am."

She rolls her eyes at him, then checks her lipstick in the rearview. She looks at me and taps her horn.

"Hang on. I'm leaving," I say, get back in the car, and fire the engine.

"Where are you going?" Julia asks.

"Parking's down the road."

"What do you want us to do?" Grady asks.

"Make the dessert table pretty. Undoubtedly, they have floral arrangements for each food stand. Start arranging the pastries." I pull the printout with instructions from my purse and glance at it. "We've been assigned a spot in the backyard. It looks like we're on the far side of the pool, adjacent to—"

Beep beep! The woman in the Mercedes hits the horn again, this time more insistent.

"Hang on," I say and edge my clunker to the side of the driveway. I stick a hand out the window and motion for her to pass.

Grady walks up to me and I roll down the window. "We're next to the gate that leads to the guest quarters." I hand him the printout.

"We'll handle it," he says. He and Julia walk toward the entrance to the side yard where all the help seems to be gaining access.

The lady in the red convertible pulls next to me and

boxes me in. She turns off her ignition, steps out of her car, and makes her way toward the house's main entrance.

"Hello," I say, exiting my car and waving. "You've boxed me in. I can't park here."

She ignores me, her chin rising a little higher with each step.

"What the—?" I mutter under my breath and reluctantly follow her.

Chapter 5

RED CONVERTIBLE

The woman who boxed me in is wearing a fabulous pair of mustard-yellow wide-legged pants, a thick, black, hip-length coat over a white V-neck cashmere sweater. She has honey-colored blonde hair. I think she's the girl who was in the photo on Mason's fridge.

"Hi," I say. "You parked right next to me. There's no wiggle room. I can't get out."

She swivels on low heels and drops her sunglasses down her nose. "You're rude."

"I'm what?"

"You're rude," she says, and tosses her keys to a valet

guy who hangs them on a little hook on his stand. He hands her a claim ticket. "I honked multiple times and you ignored me. I can't wait forever, you know."

"I did not ignore you." I feel my jaw tightening.

"You can't park there, miss," the valet says, pointing at my clunker. "You have to move, or we'll have you towed."

"I'm not *trying* to park there." My stomach clenches the way it did a few days ago when my desserts were squashed. "I'm *trying* to move my car. But I can't because this woman boxed me in."

"If you weren't so rude," the woman says, with a wave of her hand, "maybe that wouldn't have happened to you. Perhaps you should think of other instances in your life when you suffered negative consequences due to your rude behavior." She walks inside the house, her chunky heels clip-clopping on the stone-tiled floors.

I blink.

Pete walks out the front door and spots me. "Hey, Annie. You're here."

"I have to park." I point to my beater.

"Well, you can't park there," Pete says.

"I *know*," I say. "I unpacked all my desserts and was trying to move when this person boxed me in."

"What person?" Pete asks.

"Forty, somewhat attractive, mustard-pants-wearing woman. She said I deserved it because I was rude."

"Elaine," he says and eyes the valet. "Do you have her keys? Red convertible."

The valet hands them over.

"Thanks," Pete says and walks toward the Mercedes. He reaches the driver's door and pauses. "Stay away from

Elaine. She's Mason's new girlfriend. She probably saw you were cute and decided she'd better put you in your place quickly before you became a threat."

"I have a boyfriend."

"So it said on your security check." Pete takes the driver's seat, turning the ignition on. "But Elaine doesn't know that."

"My security check?" I ask.

"You signed the contract for the party."

"Yes."

"Did you read the paragraph about the background check?"

"Uh…"

"No problem," Pete says. "You passed. Something flagged from a few years back about a deceased self-help guru. Dr. Derrick Fuller? That was about it."

"Lovely," I say. "Thanks for helping. You're a peach."

"That's what they all say." He waves a hand out the top of the convertible as he moves the car and parks it yards in front of mine.

I drive past him, make a left out of the driveway, and motor down the beach lane. I go as far as I can go until the private house-lined street ends in sand dunes and boulders adjacent to a marshy lagoon.

I get out, take in the view for a second, and feel a little emotional.

"Tonight's a big night for you," Sister Cecelia says. *"Lots of potential clients here."*

"I know. Who would have thought there'd be so much drama?"

"Ignore that mean, middle-aged Elaine woman," Sister Cecelia says. *"Take a moment to breathe in the ocean air. Negative ions are calming."*

"Good to know." I take a slow inhale and exhale.

It's stunning here at the end of the street. Ocean winds are picking up, waves crashing. A few surfers are still braving it in the chilly water, waiting on their next wave. I'm tempted to take off my shoes and make my way back to Mason's house via the beach instead of the paved street. But I'd probably get sweaty and sandy, and that might not look professional. I lock my car and start walking.

"You don't have to lock your car here," Maisey says, climbing down from the top of a sand dune onto the concrete, black combat boots dangling by their laces from her fingers.

"Aah!" I slap a hand over my mouth.

"The Cross Creek community has twenty-four-seven security." She slips her boots back on and ties the laces tight.

"What are you doing here?" I ask.

"I couldn't let Mason turn fifty without me." She makes her way toward me wearing a boho-styled-below-the-knee dress and a black knit shrug. Her brunette hair hangs in loose locks, clipped off her face with barrettes. "I'm his favorite person."

I kind of doubted that. "You're going to crash his party?"

"You bet I'm going to crash his party."

"Maybe that's not such a good idea." I walk a little faster.

"It's the only one I have right now." Maisey picks up the pace and catches up with me.

"He took out a restraining order on you." I cross myself and check my watch. "You really want to do this?"

"More than anything in the world," she says.

"Why?"

"Lots of reasons."

"Give me one," I say.

"I'm a sucker for true love."

"Yeah, I don't know..."

"Believe it," she says.

"Whatever."

We walk for a solid five minutes as she prattles on the whole time. I pause about half a block before the house to catch my breath. "I've got to get to work."

"No problem," she says, pulling a blonde wig from her fringed purse.

I cringe. "I need to do the job I was hired to do..."

"Of course, you do." Maisey piles her long brunette hair on top of her head, and pulls on the wig.

"Um... I don't know if this wig thing is a good idea..." Her hairpiece is askew, one side inches longer than the other. All she needs to complete her look is clown makeup.

"What? Not the right color?" Maisey smiles up at me looking like a kid playing dress-up.

I should walk away. Perhaps I should run. Instead, my heart softens. "No, the color looks great." I reach and adjust her wig, tugging on it until it's even. "Seriously, I've got to do the job I was hired to do..."

"Understood."

"God forbid I screw this job up," I say. Maisey's wig is cute. Bob cut, platinum blonde. She looks like a different person if you didn't have an eye for detail. But I do.

"Why so nervous, Nelly?"

I shiver. "I don't know. Higher class of clientele. Bigger money?"

She waves a hand. "Your friend Grady had it right. Just picture them all naked. Unless you're Pam Anderson, or that hot actor from *Bridgerton*, the no-clothes visualization is the great equalizer."

"I got yelled at by some uptight blonde when I dropped off the desserts."

"Elaine?" she asks.

"Yes."

"Ah, the lovely, opportunistic Elaine." She applies a coat of raspberry lipstick that goes well with her outfit. "She snags Mason when he's in between girlfriends."

"What do you mean?" I check out the house's entrance. The gates are open. Guests are arriving. Based on the attire, I spot a trickle of important people, artsy people. People I should be attending to. It was a ten-minute hike back to Mason's place from where I parked my car. Maisey's presentable. Am I? I dig in my purse and pull out my lip gloss.

"Before Mason and I got together, he dated an app developer named Tina Shen. I met her. She is lovely. When they broke up, Elaine swooped in for Mason's sloppy seconds."

"Aha." I unscrew the lid on the jar of gloss and swipe a fresh coat on my lips.

"She's always had a crush on Mason."

"Was he the one that got away?"

"Away and away," she says. "A month after he started up with Elaine, Mason left her for Frankie Stewart. She used to be an Olympic athlete but she's an artist now. She is competitive and hardworking. I like her. In fact, we still talk. I saw her just the other night."

"Really?" I ask.

"Really. She texted me when Grady was giving me a ride back from your place."

"The night you set my curtains on fire."

"The night I brought you a bottle of Dom Perignon."

"Which I used to put out the fire you started," I say.

"You say to-MAY-toe," she says. "I say to-MAH-toe. Frankie's in town for Mason's birthday party. I met her at Strumpelstilskin's, a cute little bar close to the Third Street Promenade. We had a drink and caught up on old times. She couldn't believe Elaine had slithered back into his life again. She reminded me that Elaine snagged Mason literally days after they split."

"Yikes," I say. "What's with Mason's quick turnaround with girlfriends?"

"I don't know for sure." She shrugs. "Fear of being alone? Fear of dying alone? He's turning a youthful fifty, but he lost his folks when he was in his teens."

"That's tough. What happened?"

"He was staying with his grandmother in Athens while his parents took a romantic getaway to the Greek islands. They were sailing when a freakish storm popped up. Their boat capsized and they drowned."

"That's heartbreaking."

"It is," she says. "We talked about it. He opened up. Said it was the first time he's acknowledged how emotionally devastating it really was."

"Why did you guys split up?" I ask before I remembered what Pete told me. That Mason had dumped her after they got back from Aspen.

"He's scared," she says.

"What of?"

She shrugs. "What are people are always scared of? Life. Letting go. Relinquishing control."

"It's hard, isn't it?"

"Life's not for the faint of heart," she says. "And that's okay. Sometimes people confront their fears, conquer them, and move on. Sometimes they don't."

"That's a good attitude."

"I wrote about it in my book, *The Urban Witch*. It's how I deal with my own fears. In regards to Mason? He hardly ever cuts cords with his old girlfriends."

"What about you?" I ask, then wish I could reel those words back in. "Do you cut ties with old boyfriends?"

"Yes," she says. "At the appropriate time. Someone talked Mason into the restraining order. It wasn't his idea."

"Okay." I'm not so sure I believe her.

"A handful of his exes are coming in town for his party. Which is another reason I have to be there. I'm dying to catch up with Tina, and I'd like to spend more time with Frankie." She pats her wig. "How do I look?"

"Cute," I say. "Why don't you meet up with your friends *outside* the actual party. Like, on the beach, within the proper amount of yardage that your restraining order calls for."

"Then how would I be able to tell Mason happy birthday?"

I shrug. "Is it worth going to jail if you get caught?"

"I won't get caught." Maisey's already hiking down an access path that leads to the beach, her platinum-coiffed wig shimmering in the late afternoon sun as it sinks toward the horizon.

"Be careful," I call after her.

"Bye." She waves.

"I'm not sure that she knows what "being careful" means," Sister Cecelia says.

"That's what worries me," I say.

"Worry gets you nowhere," Sister Cecelia says. *"And, I'll guarantee you haven't seen the last of that one yet."*

A FEW HOURS LATER, the sun has set over the Pacific Ocean. Strategically positioned heat lamps are glowing like toaster ovens. The party is just as amazing as I hoped, and no, unlike my friend Julia, I haven't forgotten I'm a caterer and not a guest.

People mingle and chat. Hungry folks make the rounds of the food bars set up around the beachfront backyard. There's a burger stand. A taco-and-quesadilla booth. One table is loaded with a variety of salads. Moto Gear, the microbrewery, has a designated space close to the house for a selection of ales. Two small bars with wine and cocktails and soft drinks are manned by uniformed bartenders.

I'm the designated dessert person, and dare I say, based on the smiling faces of people noshing on my dessert selections, they're happy with what I baked.

"I think I saw someone I used to date," Julia says.

"That's nice," Grady says, putting out more plates on the table.

"I'll be right back," she says, shrugging off her apron.

"You're here to work," I say.

"I'll only be a minute," she says. "Besides, I'm hungry."

"Come back soon."

She makes a beeline to the burger booth a dozen yards away. She doesn't find a tuna melt but scores a great cheeseburger and is now chatting with the handsome silver-haired guy manning the table. I recognize him as Hans Swarzen, the local entrepreneur who immigrated from Austria and won a Mr. Olympia contest a few decades ago.

Mason Callaway, birthday boy, mingles with guests. Every time he leaves Elaine's side, she tracks him down like a homing pigeon and cozies up to him. She's clingy, like Saran Wrap, except for about a half hour where I don't see her anywhere.

"The people watching here is great, but it doesn't pay the bills," Sister Cecelia says.

"You're right," I mutter. "Hey, Grady, can you pass me another box of the mini cheesecakes? They're moving faster than the cupcakes."

"How is that possible?" He places another pink bakery box on the white-linen-covered table.

"I don't know." I lift the box's lid and replenish the tiered stands with sweets. "Maybe the dessert trend is changing."

Grady cleans up the crumbs on the table. He sets out more stacks of plates and napkins. "I'm in love with Mason's house, his pool."

"I haven't even had time to check out his house, or his pool yet." I replenish my stack of business cards positioned next to a dessert carousel.

"The pool has turquoise waters," he says. "It looks like the Caribbean."

I glance up. He's right. It's gorgeous. "Oh, to live this life."

"Oh, to live this life," he says and nods at the burger bar. "After I grab a cheeseburger?"

"Go," I say.

"Want anything?"

"Yes."

❧   6   ❧

Chapter 6

KICKED OUT of the PARTY

❧

"Tell Julia to come back here and put in a little work, please," I say. "The birthday cake presentation will happen soon. We'll probably be wrapping up in under an hour."

"Got it." Grady wipes his hands on a towel, then walks off.

Two women walk up to my table and peruse the desserts. One grabs a mini cheesecake and takes a bite. "Yum," she says in a German accent.

The second young woman, pretty with shiny black hair with purple streaks selects a cupcake. "Double yum."

I think these are Maisey's friends.

"Has Maisey gotten back to you yet?" The girl with the German accent picks a fruit tart from a dessert platter.

"No," the other woman says. "I texted her over twenty minutes ago. I haven't heard a peep."

"She said that she'd only be gone for five minutes," the German says. "I hope she didn't get kicked out of the party. The blonde wig doesn't fool everyone."

"Try telling her that," the other woman says. "She won't listen to me."

"Does she listen to anyone?" the German asks.

They wander away from my table.

"Should I worry?" I silently ask Sister Cecelia.

She shakes her head. *"Worry will only get you a bad ticker and a nervous tummy."*

"Right." I spot Julia making her way back to the dessert table.

Ten minutes later, the night really is winding down when Mason stops by. I introduce him to Julia.

"How goes it?" Mason selects a mini cheesecake and takes a bite.

"Good. How's the birthday?"

"Uneventful," he says. "Just like I like them. I'm not a big party person."

"Then why throw this fabulous bash?"

"To catch up with old friends," he says. "Give people an excuse to gather in person. Hey, did you see where Maisey went?"

I nearly choke. "Who?"

"Ignore that question," Sister Cecelia says.

"Pete told me that the two of you ran into each other at Moto Gear a few days ago," Mason says. "Knowing Maisey, you're probably BFFs by now."

"What would she be doing *here*?" I ask.

"It's my birthday. She never misses my birthday."

"Um..." I say.

"Come on. 'Fess up. She's wearing a blonde wig," Mason says. "Hanging out with a few of my friends. I pretended not to see her."

"Doesn't ring a bell," I say. This is *kind* of true. I didn't see Maisey hanging out with anyone at the party.

The music quiets and someone sings, "Happy birthday..." More guests chime in. In the distance, a birthday cake is rolled out on a cart, candles sparkling bright.

"They're singing your song," I say and nod in the cake's direction.

"I have to go, don't I?"

"Yes. It's your party."

He smiles and gives me a thumbs-up. He walks away but pauses and turns. "Annie."

"What?"

"Do me a favor?"

"You got it."

He smiles. "If you do happen to see Maisey? Would you tell her I want to talk?"

"Sure."

"Would you tell her that I'm sorry?"

"You are?" A hand flies to my chest.

"I am. Deeply. Profoundly," he says. "Truly."

"Okay," I say, my heart going out to the both of them.

"Thanks." He salutes, then walks toward the tiered white cake illuminated by the light of fifty flickering candles. The voices singing, "Happy Birthday" grow louder.

I realize with a pinch of guilt that my first impressions

of Maisey and Mason were premature. I thought she was a brat. Thought he might have been your typical, self-absorbed multimillionaire.

Now it seems that whatever broke them up is unresolved. This isn't an average breakup. It's not a cruel ghosting on his part. I'm starting to doubt it's about Mason dating someone else. Certainly not Elaine, Miss Bossy Pants Placeholder.

"Ooh, you don't mind if I join in the birthday cake celebration?" Julia asks.

"Do it quickly, please. I'd like someone here to help me. Where's Grady?" I ask, looking around.

She shrugs. "He delivered your message, ordered a burger, and wandered off stuffing seasoned fries in his mouth."

"Good. He needed some food," I say. "Go, but come back quickly."

"Sure, Boss." She waves and walks toward the crowd that gathers around Mason.

"I can help," Maisey says. "After all, I promised to make it up to you."

"Maisey?" I turn but don't see her. "Your friends were here a while back. They're looking for you."

"Who's looking for me?" She walks out from behind a tall potted plant a few yards away. Her wig's askew again. Her lipstick's smudged. "I doubt it's Frankie. I got in a fight with Frankie. She took off. I don't know where she is."

"What kind of fight?" I ask because she looks like she's been crying.

"Oh, just, you know..." She moves closer to me. Her boho

dress is ripped and has slipped down her shoulder. Red marks and new bruises color her upper arm. It looks like someone shook her. "Run-of-the-mill fight you have with a friend."

"Did someone hurt you?" A bad feeling curdles in the pit of my stomach. "Are you okay?"

"I'm fine, I think," she says. "Except, I don't feel like myself."

"How so?" I ask.

"I don't know, she says. "I feel a little off. I took a hit off Frankie's joint. Maybe that's it."

"Aha," I say, feeling a little relieved. Maybe she just got high. Maybe she argued with Frankie, slipped, fell, and banged her shoulder. "I don't partake, but a lot of my friends do—medicinal purposes."

"Something's not right. I feel a little light headed. I don't think it's from one tiny hit off a skinny joint. Frankie always rolls them thin. Besides, I have quite the tolerance to weed, you know."

"I did not know that." Although it comes as no surprise.

"Uh-oh," Sister Cecelia says.

"Do you know something I don't know?" I silently ask.

"Oh, Graceland." She shakes her head and walks off. *"Figure it out."*

The *Happy Birthday Song* stops, and a robust round of applause erupts. It's Mason's turn to make a speech.

"Thank you for being here," he says. "I am grateful for every person who took the time to show up tonight."

"Why wouldn't we show?" a man asks. "Great food. Great company."

"I'm not the easiest guy in the world to work for,"

Mason says. "Rumor has it I'm exacting. A bit of a perfectionist."

"Nonsense." Elaine leans up against him, preening like the cat who ate the canary. "You dot your i's and cross your t's."

"Ah, the lovely Elaine," Maisey says. "Maybe Mason dotted i's on her. That's not what he dotted on me."

I cough.

"I just want to thank everyone here tonight for being in my life," Mason says. "Thank all of you for helping me celebrate the big five zero."

"Here's to Mason," a guy says.

"Hear! Hear! Mr. Callaway," a woman says and they clink glasses.

A round of applause goes up as he blows out the candles on his cake and smiles.

The two women who were recently noshing on desserts at my table stumble through the gate which connects the backyard with the stairs that lead to the beach. "Mason," the girl with the German accent says.

He turns. "Heidi?"

The young women make their way around the swimming pool. They look rumpled and wind blown. They look shocked.

"What's wrong?" he asks and walks toward them.

"Oh, Mason." Heidi pauses poolside and draws in a shattered breath. "She's dead."

A collective gasp rises from party guests. A few hands fly to hearts. Opportunists lift their phones and film.

"Who?" Mason asks.

Heidi shakes her head, shoulders heaving. Tina puts an arm around her waist.

"Tina," he says. "What's she talking about? Who is dead?"

I peer past the bruises on Maisey's shoulder, her tear-soaked face, the disheveled wig. My gaze travels down her legs. The lower half of her boho dress is plastered thigh high, above her knees. It is soaked, dripping wet. Her shins are encrusted with sand. Seaweed wraps over her combat boots. I know what Sister Cecelia hinted at, but does Maisey?

"Do you know?" I blink back tears. Darn it, I don't want crazy Maisey to make me cry.

"That I'm dead?" she asks and turns away from me for a few moments.

I see the bloody gash seeping through her blonde wig on the back of her head. My tears trail down my cheeks, and I can't dab at them fast enough.

"We found Maisey collapsed on the beach behind a sand dune," Tina says. "She wasn't breathing.

"She's dead," Heidi says.

"That's impossible," Mason says. "She was alive earlier. She was wearing a blonde wig. I saw her."

"She's gone," Tina says. "I'm sorry."

He sits down with a thunk next to them, poolside and drops his head into his hands. "No."

They put their arms around him.

Elaine approaches, Pete on her heels. He looks shocked, his eyes round and glassy. Elaine, on the other hand, appears disgusted but determined. Like she stepped in dog poo while wearing her priciest pumps, but no matter what it takes, she's going to scrape that stuff off.

She nudges between Tina and Mason. She puts a hand

on Mason's shoulder and squeezes it. "Pete. Call nine-one-one."

"I... I..." His face is ashen.

"Pete," Elaine says, her tone gruffer. "I won't ask again."

"Right." He pulls his phone from his pocket, clicks three numbers. He walks away, a little unsure on his feet. "The nature of my emergency? I'd like to report a possible death. Yes, I'm okay. No, I didn't see it. No, I don't know what happened. The address is..."

"Wow." I sit back with a plunk on the small chair behind the dessert table. My heart is in my stomach. My head is spinning. I've got a new ghost on my hands. I have to keep it together. I owe Maisey that much. This tragic moment isn't about me. It's about her. "I don't know what to say. I don't know what to think."

"Me neither. I'm going to walk around for a bit," Maisey says, rubbing her head. "This is surreal. Kind of like getting eyeglasses with a new prescription, and you can't see that well, and then you get a headache."

"Do you need me to do anything?"

"Yes. No. I don't know?" she says, glancing around the party, confused.

"Take some time," I say, trying to find the right words. I think the simplest ones will be the best. "You know how to find me?"

"Maybe?"

"I have a feeling you'll figure it out."

"I have a feeling you're right." She wanders off, seawater dripping from the hem of her skirt.

Why didn't I convince her to skip this stupid party?

"Because you've only known her for a few days," Sister Cecelia says.

"I could have done better," I say, wiping away tears.

"She set your curtains on fire," Sister Cecelia says.

"I put them out."

"The fire department was called."

"We were all fine."

"She has no boundaries."

"Then why do I feel so horrible?" I ask.

"Because this isn't your first rodeo." Sister Cecelia says. *"And, I think in the short time you've known her, she's become your friend."*

❧

AN HOUR LATER, a handful of LAPD and Los Angeles County Sheriff's Homicide Bureau uniformed officers mill about. Guests are grouped into small clusters. Detectives interview folks one at a time while other cops poke about for clues. A few guys wearing coroner jackets cross paths as they walk up and down the narrow wooden steps to the beach.

"Clearly, I feel horrible this happened to Maisey, but I didn't see anything," Julia says. "I didn't even see her here. When can I go home?"

"Annie drove," Grady says, walking up to the table.

"I'll call a rideshare," she says. "Hell, I'll hitchhike if I have to."

"You can leave when the cops give you the go-ahead," Grady says. "After they interview the guests, they'll interview the service crew."

"It's like speed dating," I say. "The police work on first

impressions during quick questionings. They note anything weird or out of place, and move on to the next person.”

“I think they’re moving at a surprisingly rapid clip,” Grady says.

“Where did you disappear to?” I ask.

“What are you talking about?” He tidies up the dessert banquet, scraping crumbs off the tablecloth.

“Julia said you grabbed a burger at the burger stand and wandered off. What were you doing? Where did you go?”

Chapter 7

A GHOST WHISPERER

"I'm embarrassed to say that I took a self-guided tour of the house," Grady says.

"See anything out of the ordinary?" I ask.

"Other than the lack of dust anywhere?" he asks. "No. You think Maisey was murdered, don't you?"

"I'm not capable of thinking right now," I say. "I haven't eaten since noon. I feel horrible that Maisey died. I've got to fill my stomach with something other than dessert before I keel over. Then I can think. Does the burger guy have any food left?"

"Yes. Hans told me he over prepares for all these types of events," Grady says. "He never knows when someone's going to ask him to cater a spur-of-the-moment flight to an island in the Caribbean. He's handing out leftovers to anyone who needs comfort food, including servers who didn't have a chance to eat yet."

"And hungry sheriff's department personnel," I say, spotting a few uniformed officers walking away from his table, chunky burgers in hand.

"If your detective boyfriend shows up, do you think he'll let me leave?" Julia asks.

"Just a few days ago you were begging me to let you be my plus-one."

"I was hoping to meet cute, wealthy men who wanted to date a curvy blonde with a brain," she says. "Not be holed up in the backyard of a beach house in the fog waiting to be interrogated about a murder."

I sigh. "I'm sorry. Murder wasn't on my itinerary either."

"Do you think they'll assign this case to Raphael?"

"No idea." She's talking about my boyfriend, Detective Raphael Campillio. We started dating a few years back when my former husband's friend was murdered.

The dead guy, know-it-all New Age guru and best-selling author Derek Fuller, haunted me soon thereafter, vowing not to leave until I solved his untimely demise. That's how I got stuck with the most self-centered spirit in the world and also how I began my ghost-whispering gig.

I was a suspect in Derrick's death for a hot minute, and Detective Raphael was assigned to interview me. Something sparked between us, but it would have been a viola-tion of boundaries to pursue those feelings. Nothing happened in the romance department until after I was getting divorced and had figured out who killed the New Age ding-a-ling.

But even though I solved his murder, Derrick Fuller never went to the Light. As far as I know, his ghost is still walking this earthly plane, jabbering into another reluctant psychic's ear. I fear that someday, he'll resurface and haunt me again.

I remind myself to focus on the positive. Raphael and I *did* start dating after Derrick's killer was apprehended. My handsome boyfriend and I have been together for a few years, and I couldn't be happier.

"I'm going for a cheeseburger. Hold down the fort." I leave the table for the first time since I parked my car and walked back to the house with Maisey. Thoughts careen about in my brain like bowling pins that were just struck by a ball.

What happened when Maisey was on the beach? Was there some kind of fight? Was it an accident? Or did someone intentionally kill her? Did I see her murderer at the party tonight?

I venture closer toward the burger bar and don't even blink an eye when I spot Maisey's ghost wandering the party. I've been a ghost whisperer for a while now, and Malcom Gladwell's writing that says it takes ten thousand hours to master any task rings true.

I was pretty naïve my first few go-arounds with ghosts. They'd materialize and dematerialize at will, making my head spin. I'd be talking with one, turn around—and bam —that ghost would be gone. Sometimes I heard them talking loud and clear. Other times I had to lean in and really listen; it sounded like they were talking through fog. I lived in a state of being startled for almost a year.

Now I'm better at spotting the signs that a ghost is hanging around. Let me offer a few examples. Do you ever, out of nowhere, feel cold? Do goose bumps prickle on the back of your neck and all the little hairs on the back of your arms stand up for no reason? Maybe you left the front door wide open during a cold snap. Or, maybe you have a ghost in the house.

Is someone talking gibberish to you other than your drunkity friend or imaginary pep-talk coach? Perhaps you've attracted the attention of a ghost. They might love your comfy living room with the warm fireplace or simply think you're a good-hearted person who's a good listener.

You'd be surprised how many ghosts you can identify once you pay attention. People think spirit sightings are confined to crazy grandmothers or that weird woman who feeds flocks of pigeons at the park. But this isn't true. Open your eyes. Look around you. Ghosts are everywhere. Perfect example—Maisey.

She pauses next to a cluster of people huddled together, listening in on their conversation.

"I had a bad feeling about her wanting to come here," Tina says, sipping from a mug of steaming coffee. "I told her to skip Mason's party. Heidi and I would meet up with her the day after."

"But I didn't *want* to hold off," Maisey says, frowning. "I'm not the kind of person who 'holds off.' How long have we known each other? Six years?"

"I've known her for almost seven years," Tina says.

"Close enough. When we were on that beach trip to the Caymans, and Heidi asked, 'Who wants do tequila shots and dance topless on the bar with me?' Who was the first to volunteer? *Me.* I didn't hold off."

"Sometimes I thought that Maisey was reckless. That she only thought about herself," Heidi says. "Didn't care about the impact she had on others."

"Reckless? Only thought of myself?" Maisey stomps her foot. "You've got to be kidding. Remember when Frankie had a crush on that cute hockey player but his friend wouldn't leave his side? Who volunteered to distract the friend? Me."

"Do you remember when Maisey mooned those hockey players at that cute little bar in Sweden?" Tina asks. "She was so crazy."

"Ugh. I was not mooning for myself," Maisey says. "That was not a selfish act. I was mooning to help Frankie... oh, never mind. You two just aren't fun anymore. Maybe you were *never* fun." She throws her hands up in the air, bumping Tina's arm.

Tina's mug flies out of her grip and crashes onto the ground, porcelain shards flying.

"Ow," Heidi says as drops of blood bead on her forearm.

"I'm so sorry," Tina says, eyes widening. "That coffee just got away from me."

"Don't worry about it," Heidi says, dabbing blood with her fingers, her face blanching. "It's nothing."

Maisey stares at the mug's pieces scattered across the green grass. Blinking, her gaze shifts to Tina and Heidi. "Oopsi-daisies?"

"Holy moly." I cross myself. Even though I can't see Sister Cecelia, I know she's watching this too. She has to; she's my pep-talk coach. If anyone needed a pep talk, it would be me, and it would be now. *I'm calling a Code Red. What do you think?"*

"The same," Sister Cecelia says.

"That said, I know I'm not thinking clearly. I'm hungry. I'm stressed."

"Let me spell it out for you," she says. *"Maisey is a really* new *ghost. She does not have her wits about her yet."*

"I'm not sure she had wits to begin with." The scent of burgers wafts through the air.

"Maisey might have something more interesting than just wits."

"Like?" I walk toward Hans's burger booth as if on autopilot. I'm not sure if I can be more shocked tonight. Then again, never tempt the universe.

"I think your pal Maisey has poltergeist powers," Sister Cecelia says. *"She accidentally jostled her friend Tina hard enough to send a cup flying out of her hand."*

"Oh no." I shudder.

"Yup. Maisey's a poltergeist. You're in for a double-diablo roller-coaster ride with this haunting."

"Mary, Mother of God, no." I gulp and clutch my stomach and try and find a way out of this predicament. *"What if I told Maisey I can't help her? What if I told her that I have another ghost on my plate right now. That I'm only allowed to take on one at a time?"*

"Ha, ha, Graceland," Sister Cecelia says. *"That's hilarious. Once Maisey realizes your history of solving murders and sending spirits to the Light, she's going to stick to you tighter than a pair of Spanx in a size extra small."*

"I haven't sent everyone to the Light, you know. Derrick Fuller never made it to the Light." I stand at the end of a medium-length line at the burger bar.

"That windbag? Derrick Fuller lost so many brain cells

writing that New Age drivel that the light was already shining through him like he was made of Swiss cheese."

"He made a lot of money writing that stuff," I say.

"Good for him," she says. *"Look. I know you like I know how a lightning bolt feels when it courses through me. You couldn't resist solving this mystery if it walked up next to you like an alligator on a Florida golf course and bit you on the behind."*

I flinch. *"Yes, and that's what scares me. Maisey's a handful. Maisey as a poltergeist? I'm not sure I can handle that."*

"You have to. You can't turn this one down," she says. *"It's too much fun."*

"Says my imaginary pep-talk coach who has no real-life problems."

"Other than being your pep-talk coach who's at your beck and call twenty-four seven," she says. *"Besides, once Maisey gets her ghost legs, she might realize that she witnessed someone doing something hinky."*

"How so?"

"How did she get that nasty bruise on her shoulder? She said she was fighting with Frankie. Did Frankie give her the bruise? Where was Frankie when Maisey was murdered?"

"I'm not sure I know who Frankie is," I say.

"Are you still friends with Detective Google?" she asks.

"We are tight."

"Didn't Maisey mention Frankie was once an Olympic athlete?"

"Yes."

"Punch in Frankie plus Olympic athlete into Google images on your phone."

"You are so smart." Up pops pictures of Frankie Stewart. She is a cute, lithe, sun-kissed, young blonde playing beach volleyball. In another photo, an Olympic silver medal dangles around her neck.

"Find her?"

"Yes."

"Do you remember seeing her at the party?"

"No."

"I'll guarantee you're going to see her eventually."

"How so?" My stomach rumbles as I step closer to the front of the food line.

"Maisey's already haunting you," she says. *"She might have suspicions. As clever as she used to be when she was living, she was also a bit of an airhead. It's going to take time for her to take her murder seriously."*

"She didn't take a temporary restraining order seriously," I say and inhale the scent of cheese and burgers on the grill. Comfort food. *"Why would she take her murder seriously?"*

"Because once the initial shock wears off, she's going to be furious at whoever killed her. Do you think her ex-boyfriend did it?"

"Mason?" I think about it, then shake my head. *"No."*

"How is she going to feel when she realizes she's completely dead, will never get Mason back, and her concept of soul mates and true love is an illusion?"

"She's not going to be happy about that," I say—and voila—I am finally in front of the line at the build a burger table to order food.

"Unhappy people need to eat," Hans says with a German accent, snapping me from my internal dialogue with Sister Cecelia. "What'll it be?"

"Cheddar cheeseburger medium rare?" I ask. "But I'll take anything at this point."

"Cheddar cheese medium rare," he says, scooping a

cheese-topped patty from his grill. He slaps it on a thick, toasted bun. "Anything on it? Sides?"

"Hmm." This is the first time someone's served me food the whole night, and it feels like I'm in good hands. "Tomato, a pinch of lettuce. Fries."

"Seasoned?" he asks, putting together my very late dinner.

"Give her the seasoned fries and double her order, please," a man says.

I hear the familiar voice, swivel, and see my handsome boyfriend, Detective Raphael Campillio. At six feet two inches, he's a tall drink of water, on a tough day. Tears well. "You're here. I was wondering if they were going to call you out for this."

"Wonder no more," he says.

Chapter 8

A POLTERGEIST

R aphael and I sit on cushy lawn chairs on a little porch on a side patio. He'd found this space earlier when he'd poked around inside the house and talked to Mason.

"This burger's delicious," he says, wiping cheese from his lower lip with a napkin.

"I know. I can't believe I've never eaten at any of Hans's restaurants."

"How is that possible? They've been around forever. He's been around forever."

"Tonight, I feel like *I've* been around forever." I lean back, look up at the sky. Not much to see. It's a foggy night. The moon's hidden. The air feels thick and sticky with moisture. I pull my wrap tighter around my shoulders. I'm bone tired and sad.

"You knew her, didn't you?" Rafe says.

I nod. "Remember I told you about that chick who ran into me at Moto Gear?"

"The wacky one? That's Maisey?"

I nod.

"How come this doesn't surprise me," he says. "Have you told me the complete story?"

"Not yet," I say.

"Want to do that now?" he asks.

"Sure," I say, kind of, almost telling the truth. I'll happily offer up anything else that I know about Maisey when she was still alive, but I won't be sharing that I see ghosts. I'm saving *that* conversation for a different time. "Ask me anything."

"Did you know about the restraining order?" He's finished the fries on his plate and waves one finger at the ones on my plate.

I nod. "Go ahead."

"Who told you?" he asks and snags a few. "Mason?"

"Nope. Pete."

"The security guy?"

"I think that's what he does," I say. "I'm not really sure what his job entails. Security? Assistant? Driver? He met me at Moto Gear when Mason got busy and couldn't show. He drove me to the house in Marina del Rey. Took a few beck-and-call orders from Mason before he told him his workday was over and let him go."

"Got it," Raphael says.

I shiver.

"It's been a long day for you."

"The longest. But I'm good to stay as long as you want."

"I figured," he says. "Julia already asked if I would let the three of you leave the worst birthday party ever."

"Color me not shocked," I say. "You don't have to give us preferential treatment."

"I know," he says, leans in, and gives me a quick kiss on the lips. "But I like you. And you have certain traits I admire."

"Like what?"

"You always share your fries."

"Only you could coax a smile out of me after today."

"Pack your stuff. You and the crew go home. I'll get the rest of the information later."

"Thank you," I say as we stand.

He gives my shoulder a squeeze. "I'm sorry you lost a pal, Annie."

"More like an acquaintance."

"Either way it's never easy."

❧

I DON'T WANT to see Maisey's body transported to the coroner's wagon, so I'm glad we are given the all clear to leave.

When I wake up on Saturday, I check the internet ,but I don't think the news has broken yet.

I spend the day cleaning, baking, and drop off a few dessert orders in the late afternoon. Maybe the ghost of Maisey has forgotten about me. Maybe I have dodged a bullet.

"Don't count your chickens," Sister Cecelia says in the car on the drive home.

I crack the door open to my Venice Beach hovel, and am met with the whiny cries of Theodore, who seems to have forgotten I left enough food in his bowl for a fortnight.

"Yeah, yeah," I say, kneel down, and run a hand over his back and scratch his fuzzy chin. "Cat Mother loves you and she always will."

"Who is Cat Mother?" Maisey asks, and I jump.

Theodore skitters into the kitchen.

"*I* am Cat Mother." I sigh and walk into the living room. Ms. I Have No Boundaries is here.

"That's weird." She reclines on my purple velvet over-stuffed chair next to the fireplace.

"No, it's *not* weird," I say sounding somewhat resentful, even to myself. "It's normal for people to have cute nick-names for their pets."

"But it's a nickname for *you*," she says.

"Whatever," I say.

She's relaxing: head's back, blonde wig still askew, one leg draped over the fat, curved arm, her combat boot on the other, firmly planted on the seat cushion. The TV's on.

Did I leave the TV on? I wonder.

"She's a poltergeist," Sister Cecelia says.

"Poltergeists can turn on electronics?" I ask. *"I thought they just threw things."*

"Maybe she threw something at your remote."

The remote lies next to Maisey, black combat boot with the seaweed draped across it.

"It's so *brr* in here. Can you start a fire?" Maisey asks. "Maybe turn up the heat?"

"She's dripping all over your chair," Sister Cecelia says.

"She's a ghost," I silently reply.

"Boundaries, Graceland," Sister Cecelia says. *"Haven't we been working on setting boundaries?"*

"Get your foot off my chair, Maisey. The seaweed's gross. There's probably teeny-tiny dead fish or sea creatures in there still gasping last breaths. Who knows what your boot has tromped on. Beaches aren't the cleanliest places, you know."

"Oh my gosh, so cranky tonight," she says but drops her foot to the floor.

"That chair is an antique," I say, frowning. "Have you ever recovered antique furniture?"

"You mean would I ever *own* used furniture?" She shakes her head. "No, thank you, ma'am. I spring for the new stuff."

"*Antique* furniture, Maisey. It's not like I'm dumpster diving." I am not going to tell her that I've found some of my finest treasures by dumpster diving. I'm a fixer-upper at heart. I see potential in a discarded lamp that needs to be rewired, or an abandoned chest of drawers. There's almost nothing that a good can of chalk paint can't help. I'm starting to think Maisey's a bit of a snob and the less she knows about me, the better. "Recovering that chair wasn't cheap, you know. I upgraded to the high-end velvet."

"Of course. Sorry." Her eyes widen as she stands. "But now that I'm a ghost, does the seaweed even stick?"

She's got a point. I shrug. "I don't know."

We both stare at the chair where her soggy boot rested moments earlier.

"It looks okay," she says.

I run my hand over the cushion. It's dry as bone. "We're good for now."

"Great," she says and wanders into the kitchen. "Where's your guest room?"

"Guest room?" The little hairs on the backs of my arms stand up.

"Even a modest place such as this one has to have some kind of guest accommodations. I assume I'll be staying there."

"Of course, I have *accommodations*," I say, sounding like I belong on a British TV show, "but it's not really a guest room." My stomach flip-flops because Maisey's moving in with me. This is what the most determined ghosts do.

They encroach on my home, discovering their favorite space to camp out, sometimes taking over the whole apartment. They make my life a living hell until I track down their killers and find enough evidence to send to the cops.

I can't speak for other amateur psychic sleuths, but once a murdered spirit moves into my place, they hardly ever move out until I send them to the Light. It's kind of like having a roommate who doesn't pay half the rent or utilities, but for some reason they feel entitled to throw their stuff all over the living room and take more than half the shelf space in the fridge.

Some spirits are tougher to send to the afterlife than others. Over the years, I've added to my bag of getting-rid-of-ghosts tricks. It now includes tricking them, yelling at them, begging them to leave, offering a donation to their favorite charity. I once offered a free pass to Disneyland for a ghost's still-living relative.

I also use holy water, sage, prayer beads, and spells from my favorite witches. My great-aunt Stella has a few tricks up her magical, octogenarian sleeve. She used to be more active in the Wisconsin witch community but now only takes on the occasional thief, bad agent, or money launderer. She'd rather spend her time running the haunted Cheesehead Lodge in Two Sisters Bay, Wisconsin.

My cousin Izzy, who's ten years younger than me, is still an apprentice witch. She's taking Zoom classes, studying spells, incantations, and other magic. I love encouraging Izzy. She's a hard worker, brimming with raw talent and enthusiasm. But I have to be cautious using Izzy's spells; they are literally fresh out of the bag.

I cast one of her incantation about six months ago to rid myself of a particularly stubborn ghost who would not leave. Things went spectacularly wrong. Instead of ditching the ghost of Jean Pierre Montblanc, the famous Beverly Hills hairdresser who was murdered by an extremely disgruntled client, I gained the ghosts of three more hairdressers from Alabama.

They had been killed decades ago, at some kind of convention, but were still wandering the earth, looking for hair to style. They had glommed on to Jean Pierre, being that he was a celebrity and all, and were still looking for someone to solve their murders.

Suffice it to say, I've never had more hairstyling advice in my life, and I will never, ever get a perm again, so help me God, even if Jesus himself appears in my kitchen and tells me I'd look better with more bounce in my do.

I suddenly realize I don't see Maisey. Where has she disappeared to? I wander into the kitchen, but unless she dematerialized, she's not here.

Theodore has recovered from the fleeting shock of

seeing yet another ghost and is meowing in that cross tone of his when he wants me to wait on him.

I crack open a can of Tahiti Delight cat food. I spoon out crab and shrimp pâté onto his little red bowl as he weaves between my feet, head butting my ankles. I fantasize about how much it would cost to get him some kind of opposable thumb contraption and teach him how to use it. He could open his own cans of cat food, and basically become self-sufficient. I place his dish on the floor and give his round head a little scratch as he tears into his meal.

I leave my fur baby to wander down the hall. "Maisey? No answer. I poke my head in the bathroom. No Maisey. This is probably for the best. Who wants to share a bathroom with a ghost? And then it dawns on me, and my neck goes hot and then cold. I live in a one bedroom. I walk into my bedroom and see her checking out my room like a potential buyer.

"This is quaint," she says, leaning over a photo of me from nearly thirty years ago when I was nine and visiting the Cheesehead Lodge with my mom on a Fourth of July holiday.

"That was a fun weekend." I know that photo like the back of my hand.

In the background, a sagging, thick wooden pier jutted out into Lake Michigan's dark blue waters. Mom sat next to Aunt Stella in Adirondack armchairs on a grassy yard. They were sipping tall, frosty drinks.

Two picnic tables were filled with a T-shirt and shorts' crowd. Great-Uncle Elliot wore a plaid short-sleeved shirt and flipped brats on a BBQ. I was racing around the place wearing a one-piece swimsuit holding a lit, fizzy Fourth of July sparkler and wearing a big, fat smile.

"It looks like a fun weekend. Were you on a church expedition? Doing good deeds for the poor people?"

"I-I... Those are *not* the poor people," I say, shaking my head. "Those are my family and some cousins and friends of my cousins, and we were in Wisconsin..."

"Wisconsin," she says and flings herself on my bed. "The state that is known for its dells. What exactly are dells?"

"Everyone knows what dells are." I frown because I do not know what dells are. "They're those indelible things, you know, in Wisconsin."

"Right," she says and sprawls on my bed. "I love your mattress. Queen size is perfect."

"No." I feel my cheeks warm and my blood pressure rise. "No, it is not perfect. Just because you are a ghost, does not mean you are entitled to move into my place."

❧   9   ❧

Chapter 9

MURDEROLOGY

"**O**h, come on," Maisey says. "Where else am I going to go?"

"Well you had to live somewhere before tonight," I say.

"I haven't had a permanent place in years," she says. "I bounced around from nice hotel to nice hotel. My fave is the Chateau Marmont in Hollywood. I saw Leonardo DiCaprio there once."

"Maybe you should go stay with him," I say.

"Maybe you should be kinder to recently deceased persons."

"I'm sorry." I sigh. "But, you do not get to make weird

comments about my pictures, furniture, and/or my family, let alone commandeer my bedroom in this house."

"Clearly, it's not a house," she says. "But your bedroom will fit me just perfect. Thank you."

"Stick to your guns," Sister Cecelia says.

"You can't have the bedroom," I say.

"Then what are you offering?" Maisey sits up and smiles at me, cheery. "From what I've heard you're a ghost whisperer. I'm in the market for a good ghost whisperer right about now."

"Uh… "

"White lie," Sister Cecelia says.

"What kind of nun are you?" I ask.

"An imaginary *nun,"* she says.

"Whoever told you that is wrong," I say, irritated. "I am a baker of desserts. I make cheesecakes and cupcakes and fruit tarts. I have no idea where you got the notion that I talk to ghosts, but that's just crazy talk."

"I sat in the back seat of your car when you and your friends drove home from Mason's party," she says. "You being a ghost whisperer was all your friends Julia and Grady could talk about. "Do you think crazy Maisey will find out you talk to ghosts?" "Do you think Maisey who set your curtains on fire will bother you the way the other ghosts get on your nerves?""

"Oh, that." My heart sinks. She was eavesdropping on our conversation. Maisey didn't need to go out on the town to figure out I talked to dead people. All she had to do was sit in the back seat on the drive home to get the dirt. "They were talking about a TV show Grady is pitching. He's a writer, you know."

"You're a rotten liar," she says. "Seriously, I can't believe you didn't offer your services to me already. Honestly, I'm a little disappointed."

"Fine," I say. "The speaking with ghosts gig is something I keep close to the vest. I don't like talking about it."

"It's time to negotiate," Sister Cecelia says. *"You are* keeping *the bedroom. Offer her something else of value."*

"I've got an idea," I say desperately trying to think of an idea. "I'm not only a ghost whisperer. I also dabble in... murderology."

"Murderology?" Maisey asks.

I nod my head like I know what I'm talking about. "If you cooperate with me, I might be able to help you track down your killer."

"You don't think I died of natural causes either," she says. "Do you?"

I shrug. "Did you have a bad ticker? Were you stung by a bee and had anaphylactic shock?"

"But then, how did my shoulder get bruised?"

"Do you remember what happened?" I ask.

She shakes her head. "It's a blur."

"You have her," Sister Cecelia says. *"Go for the jugular."*

"Which is why I can offer you my platinum-level murderology package for the low, low price of the bronze," I say.

"Tell me more." One of her eyebrows arches.

"The platinum-murderology plan includes visiting hours at my office while we go over your case."

"You have an office?" she asks.

"A home office," I say.

"Where is it?" she asks.

"It's my desk," I say. "And an ergonomic chair."

"Fancy."

"It works for me," I say. "Platinum level also includes free rides to and from local places of interest that harbor suspects that need to be interviewed."

"Tempting," she says. "I think you can do better."

"Platinum embraces *limited* accommodations at my place while we work on your case. To be clear, this is not a *forever* deal. You do not get to live at my place *forever.* You will be expected to sign a legal document that states you understand this."

"I'm a ghost. How do spirits sign documents?"

I harrumph. "You're not the first ghost I've dealt with. Regarding the signature thing, well, I've already figured out that little fly in the ointment."

"You did?" Sister Cecelia asks.

I shake my head.

"I think the right thing to do would be to offer your bedroom to your beloved friend, who is now a newly minted, murdered person," Maisey says.

"Who's my beloved friend?" I ask.

"Me," she says. "Remember we already talked about this? We bonded the second I caught myself on your pastries."

"When you flattened them?" I scratch my head.

"That too," she says.

"Careful," Sister Cecelia says. *"She might be crazy but she's crazy like a fox."*

"Besides, giving your new ghost friend your room would cement your position as the premiere murderologist on the West Coast," Maisey says. "I'll give you five stars on Yelp."

"And last but not least, the platinum-murderology plan includes sleeping and lounging opportunities on the Hide-a-Bed," I say and for some reason, wave a hand around like I am a spokesmodel on a game show. "The extra-comfy Hide-a-Bed is tucked away in the love seat in the window nook in the living room. How's that for a deal?"

"I'll think about it." She smiles and hops off the bed. "Can I borrow your toothbrush?"

"Um…" I follow her out the door and down the hall. "You probably don't need to do that anymore."

"I've brushed my teeth at least three times a day for the last thirty-five years," she says in my bathroom, attempting to pick up my toothbrush.

At first it doesn't budge. But then the brush falls off the sink, bounces off the toilet, and lands on the tile floor. I gasp.

"I'm not about to stop now," she says, leans over and after five attempts, manages to pick it up. She raises it with two fingers, staring at it intently the whole time. She blinks at the very end, and the brush tumbles with a clatter into the sink.

"Give her your bedroom," Sister Cecelia says. *"Give it to her right now."*

"What's wrong?" Maisey asks, poking at my toothbrush. "Looks like you've seen a ghost."

"You know what? I *love* sleeping on the foldout couch," I say. "Take my room. *I insist.*"

❦

AROUND 3 A.M. I finally fall asleep. I toss and turn, images of fat burgers choked in green seaweed bounce through my head. "Medium rare with cheese please," I mumble, wake myself up and glance at the clock: 11 a.m.

I push myself out of the hide-a-bed, my lower back throbbing. I jam my fist above my waist, and dig it into the tight spot close to my hi. I limp into the kitchen and search my fridge. But there are no leftover burgers. Only desserts, some Keto protein bars, and salad.

Theodore winds around my ankles, meowing. "No, I have not forgotten breakfast." I crack open a can of Fiji Fun Fish Cat Food, and spoon out two heaping table-spoons into his poppy red porcelain dish. I pour coffee into the brown filter, flip the switch on, and almost forget about Maisey until she wanders into the kitchen rubbing her eyes and startling me.

"Your shower pressure sucks," she says.

A hand flies to my heart. "You did not..."

"Ha-ha. Got you." She stands next to the coffee pot listening to it brew.

"How'd you sleep?" I ask.

"I didn't," she says. "I explored your room."

"You did what?"

"I found your scrapbooks. You were adorable in the Junior Miss Wisconsin Pageant as Miss Oconomowoc."

"I did not give you permission to go through my room and look at my stuff." I shake a finger.

"And I found more pictures of the lodge you hang out at with the church people."

"I do not hang out at a lodge with church people."

"Whatever," she says. "The cute lodge on the lake," she says. "Why don't you tell me more about that place?"

"Don't," Sister Cecelia says. *"This is a path you don't want to go down."*

"No time right now," I say. "Later."

"Okay." She turns and wanders down the hallway.

It was Sunday, and technically I had no work today, other than a little house cleaning, hunting down Maisey's murderer, and of course warning my friends that the new ghost would unabashedly eavesdrop on our conversations and was turning into a Category three poltergeist.

An hour later I was freshly showered, wearing clean clothes, even though Maisey was right – the shower pressure did suck. I shove a few pens and a little notebook into my purse.

She waits for me by the front door, looking unsure if she should walk through it or leave the old-fashioned way. I need her gone, so I open the door, making that decision for her. "Go. It's a gorgeous day."

"Does that even matter anymore?" she asks.

"Of course, it matters," I say. "Every beautiful day matters."

"You sound like a Hallmark card," Sister Cecelia says. She's wearing a tennis outfit: a modest white skirt, a cap-sleeve top showing off her toned arms. This surprises me. I thought she was just into golf.

"What if I want to stay here and help you," Maisey says. "We could sit in your home office and investigate."

"You mean we could hang out at my desk." I shake my head. "This isn't the time for that."

"What's it the time for?"

"This is when we gather a list of the usual suspects, track them down, and figure out what they know or don't know about what happened to you."

"Got it," Maisey says. "How can I help?"

"She could help by leaving you alone for a fat minute," Sister Cecelia says, picking up my dust encrusted tennis racket that leans against the coat tree.

"Pick one of Mason's ex-girlfriends," I say. "Find her. Follow her. See if she says anything weird."

"What kind of weird thing would they say?" Maisey asks.

"I don't know," I think, watching as Theodore blinks and gets up from his patch of sunshine under the window. He stretches in downward cat and lumbers toward the open door. "'I saw Maisey on the beach talking with Ms. Mustard. Then Ms. Mustard picked up a rock on the beach, konked her head, and killed her.'"

"This is like a game of Clue."

"Exactly." I put my foot out in front of my opportunistic cat, stopping him in his tracks.

"Who should I pick?" Maisey asks.

"Doesn't matter," I say and then think about the nasty bruise on her shoulder. "Actually – Frankie. Find her first. Take your time. We'll meet up tonight at the home office --"

"You mean *rendezvous* at your desk?" she asks, a hitch in her voice.

I glance at her, once again feeling a pang of sympathy. It's so easy to be irritated with her. But with the bruised shoulder, the off-kilter blonde wig, and the seaweed sloshed across her combat boots, she looks like a little girl trying to play Halloween dress up but some bully trashed her costume. "Yes. I meant to say rendezvous. Get going."

"Will do," she says. "See ya." She de-materializes into a fine sea colored mist with a whiff of salty ocean air.

I breathe it in and immediately feel embarrassed and yet somewhat relieved. "I can live with this. It's like a day at the beach."

"If a day at the beach had a murder, a ghost who is haunting you and commandeered your bedroom," Sister Cecelia says.

"It'll be fine. Just wait and see," I say. "This will be just like any other ghost whose murder I'm tasked with solving. I'll survive this just fine — OH HOLY MOTHER OF GOD."

Chapter 10

LEMONS INTO LEMONADE

Theodore's licking a slip of seaweed on my hardwood floor and I'm not sure who will upchuck faster — him or me.

"No!" I scoop him up, but when I go to wipe the slime off his chin, there's nothing there.

He glares at me like I am a cat torturer.

"I'm sorry." I put him down and he waddles off — head down, ears back. "I thought I saw something."

His tail twitches viciously as he pads down the hallway.

"I'm *sorry*. How many times do you want me to say it?"

He ignores me and disappears into my bedroom.

I sigh.

"You can't please everyone," Sister Cecelia says.

"I know," I say, and grab a coat from my coat rack. *"It's just I wasn't expecting this."*

"Expecting what?"

"Another murder. Another ghost. If I'm being one hundred percent honest, I was really thinking Mason's birthday party would be a great venue to show off my business, not travel down this path again."

"Lemons into lemonade. It's another case for the murderologist," she says. *"Do you ever wonder if you should monetize your murderology business?"*

"No," I say, shrugging on my coat. *"That is the last thing in the world I want to do."*

"Why?"

"Because that would be giving it power. Validity. I'd be opening myself up to every quack in the world that hates ghosts or ghost hunters."

"I got a cable talk show out of my ghost talking claim to fame," Sister Cecelia says.

"I am not putting this on my to-do list, but thanks, as always, for the help."

"You're welcome. I'll send you a bill," she says.

"And I'll pay it in imaginary dollars."

❧

MY FRIENDS and I huddle around a four-top table at a coffee shop a few miles from my house on Abbot Kinney. It's a trendy, narrow street lined with expensive boutiques and eateries. I'd called an emergency meeting to discuss the blossoming Maisey debacle.

"Get out of town," Julia says, setting down her fancy iced coffee with the whipped cream with a clank.

"Not kidding," I say. "I witnessed the toothbrush levitating thing with my own eyes."

"How do you know she isn't here now?" Julia slides her sunglasses down her nose and glances around.

"I sent her off to find one of Mason's ex-girlfriends. Eavesdrop. Do a little reconnaissance. But honestly, I *don't* know. She's a ghost and they like to lurk, which is why I'm letting you know that the cat is out of the bag, the horse has left the barn, and you all need to take the appropriate measures."

"I'm not thrilled she's eavesdropping, and yet this is fascinating," Grady says, holding out his phone. His espresso cup rests next to the butter croissant he's working on. "Can I record?"

"No," I say.

He dejectedly puts his phone down.

"Not yet. I'm firming up a basic murder investigation plan," I say, taking a sip from my tall, freshly squeezed lemonade. It's not even summer yet but I had to order one after Sister Cecelia brought up the lemons to lemonade thing and put that bug in my brain. "I need to deal with that first."

"OK."

"Besides, Maisey's not your run-of-the-mill ghost. This investigation could take a weird turn," I say.

"You had me at levitating toothbrush," Julia says.

"Which would make a great visual in my movie," Grady says.

"We can discuss a movie after I solve Maisey's murder."

"Tell us about the plan," Julia says.

"The first step is to interview the former girlfriends. "There were a *lot* of old girlfriends at Mason's party."

"As well as the current one," Julia says. "The overbearing chick in the mustard pants."

"Elaine," I say.

"She was mean and snippy to the servers," Julia says.

"Agree," Grady says. "But you shouldn't have thrown a hot dog at her."

"You threw a hot dog at Elaine?" I ask.

"She deserved it," Julia says.

"Why a hot dog?"

"Mustard. Hot dogs," Grady says. "You know."

"Got it. Sorry." I dig my fist into my lower back. "My back hurts. I'm not thinking clearly." The fold-out couch has a rod down the middle that woke me up three times last night. It wasn't as comfy as I had thought.

"How do you plan to interview the ex-girlfriends?" Grady asks.

"You mean how do *we* plan to interview the ex-girlfriends?"

"We?" Julia bats her eyes, looking surprised.

"Have you ever asked for their help before?" Sister Cecelia asks.

"All the time," I silently say.

"You've never officially asked us to help you with an investigation before," Julia says.

"Yes, I have."

"Au contraire," Grady says. "You consistently reach out to us as backup. Like you're Diana Ross and we're the Supremes."

"He's right," Julia says. "This is a first."

"Then it's past time I promote you. Besides, you two are my smartest friends in all of Los Angeles."

"Flattery will get you everywhere," Grady says.

"Another reason I like you. Maisey was a handful when she was alive and she's going to be worse now that she's dead."

"Let alone a poltergeist," Julia says.

"That too," I say.

"Where do we start?" Grady asks.

"We start with Frankie," I say.

"What's her last name?" Grady clamps onto his phone like he's been handed a lifeline.

"I don't know. She goes by her first name. She's an artist." I make air quotes with my fingers around the word artist.

"Frankie was at Mason's birthday party, yes?" Julia asks.

"I think so."

"Which one was she?"

"The one I never saw in person."

Grady holds out his phone. "I found her."

We lean in and peer at the small screen. Frankie's highlighted blonde hair is piled in a sloppy updo. Her lids are smeared with copper eyeshadow and heavy cat-eye eyeliner. Her nose is pierced. Her lip is pierced. She wears a gold wrap jacket on top of a black tutu.

"She's wearing makeup from the 1960's," Julia says.

"She looks like a blonde Cleopatra," I say. "I would have remembered seeing her. My great aunt holds a Queen Cleopatra themed party every June at the Lodge."

"I think I went with you to one of those once," Grady says. "Come as your favorite goddess party?"

"Yes," I say. "I want to find out if Frankie got in some

kind of physical fight with Maisey. The bruise on her shoulder didn't look like an accident to me."

"Where do we find her?" Julia asks.

Grady taps his phone. "According to this post, she's prepping for an art show today at a local gallery."

"When does it start?" I ask.

"Now," he says.

"Why so early?" Julia asks.

"It's Sunday and Venice is sleepy on Sun..." I catch a side glimpse of a woman who looks familiar. She's tucked behind a blue and green Italian pot holding a trellis of climbing roses. Her honey-colored hair falls in front of face. She jabs the air with her finger, making her point to someone. I'd recognize that hoity-toity voice anywhere. "Elaine's here," I say.

"Get out." Julia cranes her neck. "Where is she? I don't see her."

Grady stands and glances around. "I do."

"Is she with Mason?" I ask.

"I can only see the back of the guy but I don't think so. He's sitting down but he looks tall. Metro. In his forties."

Elaine stands, dabs her lips with a napkin, and grabs her purse. "I'll be back," she says to her companion and walks through the coffeehouse's patio door.

I tug on Grady's arm. "Park it."

He's back in his chair with a plunk.

"Coincidence that she's here?" Julia asks.

I shrug. "Maybe she's going to Frankie's show. The gallery's nearby."

"Have you thought about Elaine as a suspect?" Julia asks. "Seriously. Sometimes it's not the ex-girlfriends. Sometimes it's the current ones."

"I don't know. What would she have to gain?"

"Eliminating her competition. For good."

"She can't kill everyone who used to date Mason. That would make her a serial killer and then for sure she'd get caug..." The words jumble in the back of my throat because I see Maisey.

"Hey." She waves at me from the coffee shop's front steps.

"Hey." I cough into one hand and wave with the other.

"Why are you waving at thin air?" Grady asks.

"She's not." Julia extracts a lipstick from her purse. "Maisey's here. Right?"

"Yes," I say.

Grady grabs his phone. "Do you see ghosts now, too?"

"Please," she says.

"Julia gets nervous around spirits," I say.

"I do not." She swipes on a thick coat of red lipstick.

"You're packing on that stuff like a coat of armor," Grady says.

"It's called color, buddy. It makes me look strong and healthy. I don't want crazy Maisey, the new ghost, thinking she can roll over me as easily as she just rolled over Annie."

"I did not roll over easily."

"You gave her your bedroom."

As Maisey makes her way across the patio toward us, I catch a glimpse of Elaine's male companion leaning back in a chair. He looks awfully familiar. I feel hot and fan my face.

"What's wrong?" Julia asks.

"I don't know." My neck's itchy and I scratch it.

"You're breaking out in hives," Grady says. "Are you OK?"

"Yes." I scratch harder. The man turns toward me, scrolling on his phone, and I realize why I'm having a panic attack. Elaine's companion is 'Man-Spreading' Guy.

"Oh my God, that's David Davenport sitting over there," Julia says.

"You know him?" I ask.

"Of course, I know him. I thought I saw him at Mason's party but then he disappeared. We dated for two weeks a few years back. He ghosted me for some B list actress. He's a jerk."

"He's the idiot that Maisey tripped over that first day we met at Moto Gear," I say. "This whole ghostly debacle was set in motion when I was waiting to meet Mason, but then Maisey stumbled over this creep, doused me in pale ale, and crashed onto my dessert samples."

"This doesn't surprise me," Julia says. "I wonder what he's doing here?"

Maisey waves again, walking faster. "I've got news," she says.

"That's terrific," I say. This is the happiest I've seen her since the night she set my curtains on fire. Her eyes shine. The hair on her platinum blonde wig shimmers with every exuberant step.

"What's terrific?" Grady asks.

"Annie's not talking to you," Julia says.

David moves his chair a few inches into the common walkway between the tables, the metal feet scraping on the pavement.

"I ran into Tina and Heidi having brunch," Maisey says. "And I eavesdropped."

"Aha."

"They have theories about what happened to me last night."

"I can't wait to hear them." I feel bubbly in my stomach but not in good way. I don't think she's spotted David. Maybe if we're all lucky, she won't.

"I told you I'd make it up to you some day," Maisey says. "And I never forget a promise."

David slumps back in his chair and swings one thick leg into the aisle. He man-spreads as time. Slows. Down.

Maisey trips over David's outstretched leg, hurtles through the air straight toward me, and screams. I brace for impact, hold tight to my lemonade, and holler, "Incoming!"

"What?" Grady ducks. "Where?"

"Oh no." Julia grabs her drink in one hand and her purse in the other.

Maisey crashes on the table, half sprawled, half upright, missing me by a hair.

"Holy moly," she says, pushing herself upright. "I felt a malevolent force and then next thing you know— "

"Oh, I *know*." I place my lemonade back on the table, feeling like I dodged a bullet. I glance down. Not one drop spilled. I smile. Clearly, my karma's improving, and I silently pat myself on the back.

"What do you know?" Maisey asks.

"You tripped. Don't worry about it. Happens to the best of us," I say.

"Maisey's here, isn't she?" Grady asks.

"Yes."

"That doesn't explain the malevolent force," Maisey says, righting herself.

Elaine walks up to the table and reclaims her seat

across from David. "Ready to talk to Mason about my plan?"

"Sure," he says, standing.

"Wait a minute. I recognize that voice." Maisey turns and does a double take. "What is Elaine Schnitzel doing with Mason's money manager?"

"Huh?" I ask.

Chapter 11

A SECRET GARDEN

❦

Grady fidgets. "What did Maisey say?"

I glare at him. He's like the kindergartener who can't lie still on his mat during nap time.

Julia, on the other hand, plays it cool. She slides her sunglasses down her nose, slips her phone from her purse, and clutches her fancy iced coffee with her other hand. The only thing betraying her nervousness are her white knuckles clenched around the frosted mug. "What *did* Maisey say?" She lifts the drink to her crimson lips.

"'What is Elaine Schnitzel doing with Mason's money manager?'" I say.

"What?" She spits out her beverage. The frosted mug

slips from her grip, bounces off the table, and splatters me with iced coffee and whipped cream.

"Oh no," I say.

"Oh man," Grady says.

"I'm sorry," Julia says.

"Oopsi-daisies," Maisey says.

❧

WE TAKE a detour to my place so I can clean up. Forty-five minutes later, my friends, Maisey and I arrive at Frankie's show at Vida V gallery.

The shop is urban rustic and pretty. Situated next to a greasy car repair place, the gallery is housed in a Venice bungalow tucked behind a bougainvillea-covered iron gate. The sun pokes through a few clouds as we make our way past a line of parked cars waiting for new brakes and tires.

"I still can't believe David Davenport is Mason's money manager," Julia says. "He's making a pretty penny, yet he insisted we go Dutch on our dates."

"Cheap is cheap," I say.

We enter an oasis filled with flowers and plants. Brightly painted picnic tables are adorned with crystals, cacti arrangements, and table art. It feels so Zen here and I take my first deep breath since I saw Maisey headed across the coffee shop patio.

"It feels like we walked into a secret garden," Julia says.

"Agree," Grady says.

We move past a cluster of folks bottlenecked at the gallery's entrance and enter the space. It features fifteen foot tall ceilings and white walls, hung with bright paintings. Handmade pottery is displayed on trestle tables.

Price tags are small and discretely positioned, but I suspect the actual prices are not.

A twenty-something, cheery brunette in a long, flowing dress directs attendees to add their names and emails to a clipboard that has been placed on a narrow desk. We do as she asks. The late Sunday afternoon art crowd is a mix of casually attired upscale, wandered-in-off the street people, and a few actors.

"Check it out," I say. "The woman talking to that guy at the far end of the room next to the large orange and yellow abstract oil painting. Is that Frankie?"

"The pretty blonde with the Cleopatra styling?" Julia asks.

"That has to be her," Grady says.

The man she's talking to turns. Mason. He's aged ten years since last I saw him. Dark circles rest under his eyes. He hasn't shaved. He appears exhausted.

"What's birthday boy doing out so quickly after the murder?" Julia asks.

"We don't know for sure it's murder," I say.

"Ghosts don't haunt you unless they've been murdered," Grady says.

"Agree," Julia says. "Why's he here?"

"Mason doesn't sit around all by himself with uncomfortable feelings whispering in his ear," Maisey says. "Feelings make him nervous."

"A lot of people are like that," I say.

"Like what?" Grady asks.

"She's talking to Maisey again," Julia says. "Just assume that when Annie's talking to herself, that she's actually conversing with her new ghost."

"They are not *my* ghosts. I do not collect ghosts."

"Slain spirits find you and nag you to solve their murders. Shall I go through the list?" Julia asks.

"There is no list."

"Liar. Number one. Derrick Fuller. Killed with a poisoned cupcake. That ding-a-ling new age guru started haunting you when you mistakenly conjured him with one of your grandmother's spells at the Pacific Shrine."

"That was a mistake," I say. "That was my first time using a spell."

"Two. Edith Flowers, sales lady from Snotsky's Department Store was strangled in the store's changing room. She started haunting you minutes later in the ladies lounge because you were her last customer before she was killed. Number three— "

"Stop," I say.

"Fine." Julia sniffs. "For what it's worth, if you're going to snoop about and investigate who killed Maisey, you might not want to call attention to yourself by being the sweetest smelling person in the room."

"Huh?"

"I smell caramel coffee and it's coming from you."

"Impossible," I say. "We swung by my place so I could shower."

"That's nice," she says. "Did you shampoo?"

"No." I try not to sound irritated. "You were yelling at me to hurry up."

"Next time, shampoo."

"Next time, don't douse me with your fancy drink."

"I get that you're crabby," she says. "You're always crabby when a new ghost pops up."

I roll my eyes. "Fine. Yes. You're right."

"Your friend is judgmental," Maisey says. "Do you want me to try and throw something at her?"

"No."

"*I'm* sorry," Julia says. "Maybe I'm coming across as too harsh. I'd be irritated too."

"Ditto," Grady says.

"I'm going to go check out the Pueblo pottery. Meet up with you later." Julia wanders to the right.

"I'm going to go say hi to Mason," Maisey says.

"Do you think that's a good idea?" I ask.

"Yes." She walks to the left.

I sigh, crack my neck, and then follow her.

"Where are you going?" Grady asks.

I pause. "I'm chaperoning you know who. Want to join me?"

"In a bit. I just spotted Evan Randall." He bounces up and down on his heels. "I'm so excited!"

"Who's Evan Randall?"

"The director on that TV show I love."

"Which one?"

"The one with the wacky family that lives in a haunted house and solves murder mysteries."

"That sounds familiar."

"Because it sounds like your family?"

"Kind of." (See The Case of the Sugar Plum Shenanigans.)

"Go do your amateur sleuthing, murderology thing," he says. "I'll meet up with you later."

"'K."

Thirty seconds later, Maisey's standing between Mason and Frankie, eavesdropping on their conversation. I position myself a few yards away and pretend to study a painting.

"Annie," Mason says.

I turn and feign surprise. "Mason. What are you doing here?"

"The artist is a friend of mine." He introduces me to Frankie. "Annie was in charge of the dessert bar the other night."

"I never made it to the dessert table but I heard everything was fabulous," Frankie says.

"Thanks." I point to the painting. "This is your work?"

"Yes."

"It's gorgeous. The colors blend, and yet they hold their own. I could see this inside the house of someone who loves the beach. Someone who loves being bathed in sunlight."

"You called it," Frankie says.

"Join us," Mason says, and I do.

"Are you happy with the turn-out at your show?" I ask.

"Yes," Frankie says, "considering I almost canceled after Friday night's tragedy."

"It's unbelievable. "I'm in shock." Just then, I spot Elaine at the entrance. She bypasses the sign-in table and hustles toward us.

"Me too. Did you know Maisey?" Frankie asks.

"Briefly."

Elaine pushes in between Frankie and Mason separating them with one practiced maneuver. "Hi, hi." She clutches Mason's arm, stands on tip-toes, and kisses him on the cheek. "Sorry, I'm late, sweetie."

"You didn't have to come," Mason says. "I expected you to spend the rest of the weekend with your mom."

"Mom, the perpetual worry-wort, is fine," Elaine says. "Why are you here? Shouldn't you be resting in Malibu?"

"I couldn't stay in that house," Mason says. "I left."

"What do you mean you left?"

"I left."

"She didn't stay with him on his birthday weekend?" Maisey asks. "What kind of girlfriend is she?"

I bite my lip because I think I know the answer to that.

"Where'd you go?" Elaine frowns.

"To the Marina house."

"When?"

Frankie studies her shoes.

"Early Saturday morning, after you got the panicky phone call from your mom."

"I knew I should have stayed with you," Elaine says. "You were in shock. My God, Mason, Pacific Coast Highway is dangerous. You could have gotten into an accident."

"I didn't drive," he says. "Pete did."

"Well, that's a relief. Thank God we have Pete. He's a loyal soldier." Elaine rubs Mason's arm. "You could have messaged me, sweetie. I would have picked you up."

"Who would have taken care of your mom?"

"I would have called David. My cousin needs to spend a little less time managing your money and a little more time with his beloved aunt. Why don't we cut this outing short and go home?"

Mason frowns. "But I don't want to go home."

"We can order in. Open a bottle of wine. Relax in the Jacuzzi."

"Ew." Maisey stomps her foot, clipping Elaine's shoe.

"She's using my Jacuzzi."

Elaine winces and glances down.

"No," Mason says. "I'm here to support Frankie."

"Greatly appreciated," Frankie says.

"I think it's too soon for you to be out socializing," Elaine says.

"Since when is she the boss of him?" Maisey asks. "Anyone who knows Mason knows he'd be dying to get out of the house. Sitting home with all those emotions wears on him."

"I agree," I say.

"That it's too soon to be out socializing?" Elaine turns her attention to me.

"No. I agree with…" What *do* I agree with? "Supporting Frankie. That's why I'm here, too."

"Thanks," Frankie says.

"Maisey and I had our differences. But I never could have predicted yesterday's tragic events," Elaine says. "Do you think that maybe, perhaps, oh, I don't know, Maisey was *depressed?*"

"What?" Maisey says, balling her hands into fists.

"Absolutely not." Frankie shakes her head. "I talked with her at the party. She was feisty and opinionated and wouldn't shut up."

"Same old Maisey," Mason says. "Now I feel even worse that I took out that stupid restraining order against her."

"I knew it," Maisey says. "I *knew* it wasn't his idea."

"Mason, we talked about that," Elaine says. "The restraining order was part of you learning how to set boundaries with her."

"I know how to set boundaries," he says, the muscles in the angle of his jaw popping.

"Not with Maisey. She wouldn't leave you alone. She trespassed. She broke in. She texted you constantly. She wouldn't take 'No' for an answer."

"Let's *talk* about boundaries," Maisey says. "Elaine got pissed when I told Mason he needed a detailed analysis of the funds his money manager, *her cousin,* collected and invested."

"There are other ways to set boundaries," Mason says.

"Sugar, you tried the other ways," Elaine says. "You even had Pete talk to her."

"Pete *tried* to talk to her," Mason says, "but didn't get anywhere. Maisey got mad and hung up on him."

I shoot a look at Maisey. "Why did he ask Pete to— "

"They used to date," Frankie says. "That wasn't the smartest idea, Mason."

"Why not?" Mason looks irritated. "They were still friends."

"You don't get it." Frankie shakes her head. "Women do *not* like ex-boyfriends telling them what to do."

"Ding. Ding. Ding," Maisey says. "I hadn't dated Pete in two years. Even when we were together, I didn't let him tell me what to do. Maybe if Mason had just *listened* to me, he wouldn't be bleeding money, and I'd still be alive."

"Mason's bleeding money?" I blurt out.

"Excuse me, do I *know* you?" Elaine looks angry enough to pop me. "Have we met?"

"Yes," I say, not surprised she doesn't remember being a jerk to me just a few days ago. "I'm Annie Graceland. The dessert caterer at Mason's birthday party."

"I don't want to talk about this anymore," Mason says. "It's Frankie's special day. Mine was Friday."

"And look how well that turned out," Maisey says.

$\mathscr{H}$ 12 $\mathscr{H}$

Chapter 12

I HEART MALIBU

$\mathscr{L}$

"Y ou're right. Calm down. Everything's fine." Elaine squeezes Mason's arm and turns her attention to Frankie. "Did I ever tell you what a talented artist you are?"

"I don't think so," she says.

"Well, you are. You've really improved over the years since I've known you."

"Thanks?" Frankie cringes.

"All hail, Elaine, queen of the passive aggressive compliment," Maisey says.

She's right, and I cringe a little, too.

Frankie fidgets, her gaze lighting on a few people congregated around her paintings. She glances at Mason.

"Great talking with you. Sorry. I need to go hang with other guests."

"Of course," he says. "Go."

"Nice to meet you, Annie. Good to see you, Elaine."

Elaine tugs on Mason's shirt sleeve. "I'm dying to see the Pueblo pottery." The two head off.

"Are you thinking what I'm thinking?" Maisey asks.

"What is Elaine hiding regarding her cousin, the man-spreading money manager?"

"Yes. I told Mason there was something off with his financial statements almost a year ago."

"What were you doing looking at his financial statements?"

"I look at everything," she says.

A chill zips down my spine. I'd bet money she's snooping through my stuff too. "You said that you ran into Tina and Heidi."

"I found them having brunch at Le Blanc, my favorite bistro on Melrose."

"Brunch at a French café two days after you died is a little cold."

"They're not the warmest people."

"You said they had a theory about what happened to you."

"Tina thinks Elaine was trying to eavesdrop on my conversation with Frankie during the party. Heidi saw Elaine leave the house well before the birthday cake was wheeled out. Their money is on Elaine."

"Do you think Elaine could be a killer?"

"You're the murderologist. What do you think?"

"What's her motive?"

"Other than being thoroughly unpleasant with

sporadic bouts of kindness?" Maisey shrugs. "I don't know."

"How did you know her?"

"She came to my book signing when I launched *Urban Witch*. I contributed to a charity she recommended."

"Which was?"

"Save the Bumblebees? Save the Turtles? Save the—"

"Yeah, yeah, I get it."

"What do we do next?" Maisey asks.

"Gather more information." I glance around. Foot traffic has picked up and the place is busy for a Sunday afternoon show. "I'm going to mingle."

"I'll eavesdrop," she says. "I'm getting pretty good at it."

"So am I."

AN HOUR later I've chatted with or listened in on just about everyone's conversations in the gallery. My head is spinning with art scene gossip, new faces on the horizon, trends, and price tags.

But none of that matters, because I'm not here because I'm an art show groupie, nor do I have the spare change to plunk down on a pretty, over-priced painting. I'm here to figure out what happened to Maisey.

"*Who's on your list of suspects?*" Sister Cecelia asks. She's popped up, and is checking out a few of the paintings. She's swapped out her tennis gear for a chunky, black motorcycle jacket and mom jeans. They go great with her shortish silver- white hair and the rosary she clutches.

"*Who isn't, might be a better question.*"

"I'll bite," she says. *"Who isn't?"*

"Mason Callaway. I just don't get the murderer vibe from him."

"Anyone else?"

"Me and my friends."

"Your judgmental blonde friend doesn't seem to like Maisey all that much," she says.

"Not liking someone and killing them are different stories."

"Who are your top suspects?" She eyes a large black and white framed photograph. It features penguins migrating on Arctic ice and is titled "The March of the Nuns."

"Too soon to call," I say. *"I don't like Elaine, but that might be a personal thing."*

"Why in the world is Mason dating her?"

"I don't know, Familiarity? A place-holder until the next almost –right girl comes along?"

"Speaking about suspects," she says, *"talk to me about ex-girl-friend Frankie. Did you find out anything about the argument she had with Maisey?"*

"A rumor's going around that Frankie and Mason might be getting back together."

"Who'd you hear that from?"

I point to the upscale group of guests hanging out with Frankie.

"They were whispering about it right in front of her?" Sister Cecelia asks.

"No, Frankie quietly mentioned it to one of her friends. Nothing's happened yet because Mason and Elaine are still together."

"Elaine's not going to be happy about this," Sister Cecelia says. *"Do you think she killed the messenger?"*

"Maisey?" I shrug. *"I don't know."*

"What about Maisey? Maybe she wasn't happy either. Do you think she and Frankie had a fight?"

"I don't know. Both of them were ex-girlfriends. It's not like anyone except Elaine had current dibs on Mason."

"How long does he go between girlfriends?"

Mason's talking to the receptionist at the front of the gallery. The trendy, twenty-something brunette flirts and hands him a white envelope that I'm pretty sure contains a bill of sale and a certificate of authenticity for Frankie's 'Sun Dropping Toward Horizon' painting. I hope he's not going to skip over Frankie and find the next new girlfriend.

"From what I understand, not that long."

"Men," Sister Cecelia says. *"To be honest, it wasn't that diffi-cult deciding to become a nun. New topic. What are the killer's motives?"*

"One. Money." I point to Mason who's handing a check to the shop attendant.

"Come to Jesus money." Sister Cecelia clutches her rosary a little tighter. *"He's got it. Everyone wants it."*

"I have a feeling Elaine's cousin, the money manager, might be skimming some of it."

"That gives me the shivers," Sister Cecelia says. *"Murders are usually committed for money, power, or passion. Go forth and gather more information, Graceland. I'm out of here."*

"Where are you going?"

"Biker meet-up at Saddlepeak Lodge in Malibu." She dons an imaginary helmet.

"You're kidding me, right?"

"I rarely kid, kiddo," she says, almost unrecognizable in the headgear. *"But you already know this."*

"Have fun." I wave as she walks out the door. *"Be careful."*

She waves back, and then like any other imaginary pep-talk coach — poof — she's gone.

Ten minutes later, I'm exhausted from all the chatting and the eavesdropping. I buy a cactus arrangement in a pretty hand-made pot to support Vida V because I want to support local businesses.

I meet up with Julia and Grady at the front of the shop. We head outside where I plunk down at a brightly-colored picnic table. The sun is dipping. I put my feet up on the bench, kick off my shoes, and rub my foot. "Jeez, those concrete floors are hard."

"Find out anything useful?" Grady asks.

"Maybe."

"Anything you can take to the cops?"

"Slow down, Batman." I move to my other foot, jamming my thumb into the instep. "I'm not that quick. Give me more than 24 hours, 'K?"

"'K," he says.

"We're leaving," Julia says. "You coming?"

"No."

"You're going to stay here all alone?"

Maisey takes a seat opposite me. "Am I really alone?" I waggle my eyebrows.

"Talk later." Julia rolls her eyes. "Don't let your new BFF set anything on fire."

My still breathing friends exit the secret garden, disappearing through the line of parked cars still waiting patiently for new brakes and oil changes. Mason and Elaine exit the gallery. I turn away from them and pretend to talk on my phone.

"Annie." Mason waves a hand.

"Yes?"

"Either Pete or I will get hold of you in the next few days. Another short-notice gig if you're up for working it."

"Very short notice," Elaine says. "I think it should wait."

"That sounds good to me," I say, curious.

"You're the best," Mason says.

Elaine tugs on his arm as they walk away. "I thought I was the best."

"Of course, you are," he says as they exit the parking lot.

"I still can't believe he's dating Elaine," Maisey says. "*Again.*"

"I'm with you on this one."

"Did you find out anything useful?"

"Yes. I think Mason just bought one of Frankie's over-priced paintings."

"I expected he'd do that. Anything else?"

"Elaine's cousin Dave, aka Mason's money manager, is probably cooking the books and skimming from Mason's fortune."

"I suspected that almost a year ago. No one listened to me. And?"

"I hate standing on concrete floors for more than two hours in a row, but perhaps the saddest news..."

"What?" She cocks an eyebrow.

"I still don't have a clue who wanted you dead."

She sighs. "Neither do I."

THE NEXT DAY, Maisey and I return to the Malibu beach. It's overcast; not a spot of sun poking through the clouds.

Mason's house is in a gated community and I'm no longer on the guest list. I park on the side of the road and hike down to the beach via the first public access staircase that I find. It's not raining on land yet, but a few clouds further out over the ocean are opening up and spilling a flurry of drops.

Mason's house might be private property but the beaches are public. We walk on the sand to his place, then turn and make our way to where the beach narrows and the tallest boulders make it impossible to walk around them during high tide.

Yellow crime tape cordons off the short sand dunes where Maisey's body was found. I'm tempted to slip under the tape and poke about, but realize that's a foolish idea. Undoubtedly the police already searched the area for evidence.

Besides, Maisey doesn't have too many memories of the night she passed away. If I don't push her, don't trigger her, they might come back on their own. Now she tries to pick up stones and throw them into the ocean.

I plunk down on the sand and percolate.

"Why are you frowning?" Sister Cecelia asks. She's seated next to me, wearing board shorts, Ray-Bans, and a sweatshirt that says, "I Heart Malibu." Her white hair's secured high in a short ponytail. She drops her metal detector. *"What's going on in that brain of yours?"*

"I'm looking for clues but I'm not sure what, if anything, I'll find. The surf washes just about everything away. Undoubtedly the police combed the area. Your metal detector's imaginary, yes?"

She shrugs. *"I can't give away all my secrets."*

"I'm doing it, Annie. Watch me." Maisey yells.

"OK."

She picks up a pebble and hurls it toward the ocean. It flies a few feet and lands in the water with a plop.

"Not bad for a new poltergeist," I say.

"Yay!" She punches her fist in the air.

I fake a smile. She'll forever have that bruise on her arm, the platinum blonde wig that's askew, mascara-stained cheeks from crying, and seaweed on her shoe. She'll forever be a hot mess.

"I can't get a handle on what happened to Maisey," I silently say to Sister Cecelia.

"How so?"

"I don't really have any clues as to who would want her dead. She's a character. A touch of crazy mixed with a bucket of smarts. She'll charm you one second. The next she's saying or doing something ridiculous or foolhardy, and you want to throttle her."

"That's a clue," Sister Cecelia says.

"What do you mean?"

"Match Maisey's eccentricities with someone who couldn't deal with them."

"I fear that might be everybody."

"Narrow it down to someone who had access to her at the party. Someone trying to hide that fact. That might give you more insight, murderologist."

"That's the first time you've called me murderologist."

"Do you hear the lemons being squeezed, Graceland? You're making lemonade. That's what the best ghost whisperers do."

❃   13   ❃

Chapter 13

THE URBAN WITCH

🖎

Late afternoon the next day I sit across the kitchen table from Raphael Campillio, my handsome boyfriend. He wears jeans and a long-sleeve, fitted T-shirt that hugs the muscles in his arms, making them look delectable. I brought home a plate of freshly baked cookies from Feinberg's Famous Deli, the restaurant where I work part-time. It rests on the Formica tabletop between us.

After much pleading, I was able to convince Maisey to leave my place for a few hours so I could spend quality time with Rafe. Except for Theodore, who's sitting on his lap purring contentedly, we've got the place to ourselves, but I don't know for how long.

"Tell me more about the Maisey investigation," I say, munching on a sugar-encrusted sweet.

"Not that much to tell," he says.

"What was the cause of death?"

"That hasn't been released to the public yet." He dips a cookie in a frosty glass of milk and takes a bite. "Therefore, I can't tell you."

"I think I know." I saw the bloody gash on the back of her blonde wig.

"How?"

"Gossip."

"Who's gossiping?" A scattering of crumbs rests on his full lips.

"Everyone." I softly brush the crumbs away.

He smiles. "Thanks."

"You're welcome. I went to an art show on Sunday. Frankie, one of Mason's ex-girlfriends, had an exhibit. Mason and Elaine, his current girlfriend, showed up."

"I already interviewed Mason and Elaine."

"The night of the birthday party?"

He nods. "I plan on doing it again. Did you know Maisey before that day she ran into you at Moto Gear?"

"No, but I did learn a few things before she died."

"Like?"

"She came across as ditzy. But peek behind that cotton candy exterior, and she's feisty, determined, and smart. You know that she used to date Mason."

"Who didn't date Mason? He'd taken a temporary restraining order out on her."

"I know, and yet she showed up at his house last week when he interviewed me for the catering gig at his party."

"She did?" he asks, looking interested.

"Yes."

"Does Mason know this?"

"I don't think so, but there are security cameras everywhere in that place. Undoubtedly, every angle of that place is taped." My throat tightens as I remember staring up into one when I was snooping.

"So when I review the footage will I find video of you doing something you weren't supposed to be doing?"

"Maybe." I shrug. "Okay, fine. I might have gotten a little lost on my way back from the bathroom and taken a wrong turn. Got any information to throw in my direction? Clues?"

"Why do you need clues?"

"Because I love true crime shows and I'm an armchair sleuth."

"Right," he says. "Here's your clue. Look for things about Maisey Miller that are already in the public record."

"Like?"

"What did your pal Maisey do for a living?"

"She wrote a book called *The Urban Witch* and she wasn't my pal."

"Her book was a bestseller?" He grabs another cookie. "She made millions off it?"

"Doubtful."

"What did she do to pay the rent?" he asks, taking a bite of the sweet. "You know. Keep the lights on."

"I don't know."

He takes a sip of milk. "Why don't you Google her and find out?"

"Why don't you throw me a bone?"

"Maisey didn't live off her book money. She was an heiress."

"Get out."

"Public record, Annie Graceland, is the armchair sleuth's biggest friend. Maisey's parents passed away a while back. She was an only child. She inherited a substantial chunk of change."

"Huh," I say. "I'm going to have to think about this. Anything else?"

"Nope." He looks pointedly at the plate resting between us. One cookie left. "You take it."

"You take it."

He leans across the table and kisses me. "Want to split it?"

My heart pitter-patters. "That works."

He sets Theodore on the floor and pushes his chair back from the table. He picks up the last cookie, cracks it in two, and holds one piece out to me.

"Thank you." I stand and take it.

"You're sweeter than the cookie." He pulls me to him and kisses me.

This man. This handsome, sexy, sweet, kind man.

We kiss for a while. And then sometime later, thirty seconds or five hours, I don't know, I lost track of time, we stop. I remind myself to breathe.

I still have that cookie in my hand, so I bite into it. "So basically, by offering to split the cookie with me, you're confirming that Maisey was murdered."

"Where'd you get that idea?" He bites into his and smiles.

"We've been together three years. I know you, Raphael Campillio. I've cracked *your* secret code."

"I love you." He tucks an errant lock of hair behind my ear. He reaches for my hand and leads me out of the kitchen, down the hallway toward my room. We stand in front of the door to my room and he kisses me again.

I gaze up into his chocolate brown eyes. Goosebumps erupt on the backs of my arms. "I love you back."

❧

A FEW HOURS later I kiss my delicious boyfriend goodbye. I plant myself at my home office, otherwise known as my desk with the ergonomic chair. I type in "Maisey Miller" into the Google search tab and startle a little as headlines with links start popping up.

"Maisey Miller at *Quincy is Gone* movie premiere."

She's posed on the red carpet next to a few actresses I've seen on TV. I'm used to seeing Maisey in a platinum bob wig, but in this photo her long, shiny brunette hair is sectioned back in diamond clips. Her green dress is whimsical.

"Maisey Miller at *The Urban Witch* book signing at The Last Bookstore."

She's holding her book and beaming as fans lean in around her.

"Maisey Miller and Mason Callaway attend Greenpeace Fundraiser at the Getty Villa."

She and Mason are posed on the steps of The Getty Villa looking cozy and elegant. She's dressed in what appears to be a vintage gown. The fine print in the article confirms the dress is a 1972 Chanel.

And then there are the gossip-y links associated with every pseudo-celebrity:

"How Much is Maisey Miller Worth?" "When did Maisey Miller's Parents Die?" "Is Maisey Miller an Only Child?" "Is Maisey Miller Married?" "Did Maisey Miller Die?"

Oh yes, Maisey's an heiress, all right. Why did I even entertain the idea that a book called *The Urban Witch* could pay her bills in today's market? Why didn't I know she had money just by looking at her? She wore whatever she wanted. She did whatever she wanted. She said whatever she wanted.

I power down my computer. This whole time I've been thinking someone wanted to off Maisey because she was a persistent, irritating fly in the Mason Callaway vat of money ointment. But maybe someone murdered Maisey for different reasons.

"I'm home, honey," Maisey announces. She materializes, making her way through the living room, *clomp-clomp, squish-squish.* Her boots squeak on my wooden floor.

"Where'd you go?" I ask.

"I don't really know," she says, pausing. "But it was festive and it was outdoors. Food and drink were involved but I didn't get to partake, of course. Oh, Tina and Heidi were there."

Theodore purrs and weaves around her ankles. I beckon to him but he ignores me. *Great.* My cat likes Maisey more than me.

"Did you have a nice time with the boyfriend?" she asks.

"Yes," I say, pitching the pillows off the fold-out couch. "Thanks for the privacy. Did you find out anything?"

"Tina wants to know if and when someone will have an estate sale. She wants my vintage Chanel dress and the matching pumps. Heidi wants the Dior and the Halston."

"That's it?" My jaw clenches in anger. "The warmest thing they could say about you was that they want to buy your vintage clothes?"

"Tina started a Google spreadsheet so they could keep track of what they wanted to bid on. Heidi's going to make a donation to my favorite charity in my honor."

"I like the donating to charity thing more," I say. "I'm sorry they're so... mercenary."

"Me too. I'm going to call it a night." She continues down the hallway.

"Night," I say.

"Hey Annie?"

"Yes?"

"Thanks for being my friend."

❧

LATER THAT NIGHT, I toss and turn on the hide-a-bed from hell while Maisey hangs out in my bedroom. When I'm asleep I count sheep, and think about how silly this whole set-up is. I'm slumbering in the living room like a college student who crashes at a friend's pad, while Maisey's ghost is luxuriating, doing God-knows-what, in the privacy of my room.

New, weird friendships aside, she's a spirit. She can't

enjoy the high-density foam mattress I bought a few years back. I desperately hope she's unable to try on the soothing, sleepy-time eye mask that hangs from the post on my bed frame. The benefits of the white noise sound machine are probably lost on her. Perhaps she's whittling away the time going through my clothes or other stuff. I doubt she'll find anything all that interesting.

The next morning after my shower, I brew a wickedly strong pot of coffee, slip a sliced bagel into the toaster oven, and feed Theodore "Meaty Beefy Big and Bold Cat" kibble, which he promptly turns up his nose at. "This is not a three-star Michelin joint. Eat."

He meows half-heartedly and waddles away.

I lift him up under his armpits, plunk him back down in front of his bowl, and tap a finger on it. "Eat."

He glares at me, but then he does.

Maisey takes a seat at the kitchen table. "Your cat's adorable. I think he likes me."

"I know." I pour two mugs of sludgy coffee and place one in front of her.

Her eyes widen. "Oh, how I miss coffee."

"Oops, I'm sorry." I return the mug with a nervous clatter to the kitchen counter. "It's kind of a reflex."

"I'll get over it," she says. "I checked out your bulletin board last night. Great photos."

"Thanks... Hey, wait. My bedroom doesn't have a bulletin board." I remove the toasted bagel from the oven and drop it on a plate.

"Not your bedroom. The one in your home office."

"My home office?" I slather cream cheese on it and take a bite. "You mean the bulletin board that's hanging over my desk in the ...living room?"

"Yes."

"I lent you my bedroom," I say, feeling irritated. "I'm roughing it on the hide-a-bed. *Ew.* You were watching me sleep?"

"No." She scrunches her nose. "Don't make me sound like a stalker."

"Let's talk about that," I say and take a sip of coffee. "Now's as good a time as any to bring this weird tidbit up and hopefully clear the air. "The day we met, you showed up uninvited at Mason's Marina del Rey house and helped yourself to his hot tub. Persons might construe that as stalking."

"I still had a key to the property and my back gets a little achy now and again. Other persons might construe that as self-care. Why would I go to some random germy place when I can just pop by Mason's pad?"

"There was a restraining order against you."

"Undoubtedly at Elaine's insistence," she says. "I do not like that woman."

"Does anyone like that woman?"

She holds up a hand and we high five.

"I saw more pictures of you at that cute lodge," she says. "Who are the people?"

"Show me."

She walks into the living room and I follow her. She points to a photo pinned on the board. "This one."

Chapter 14

WEIRDO HABITS

gaze at a polaroid so old, it's edges are bent. It's like peering back in time — a trip down nostalgia lane at an outdoor winter party at the Cheesehead Lodge. A Christmas tree sparkles with red and green lights. Uncle Elliot's dressed as a tall elf in a green suit, a goofy hat, and weird shoes. My cousin Izzy, a toddler in this picture, is bundled up in a chunky snowsuit that makes her look like a Tootsie-roll.

"That was a Christmas festival at Great Aunt Stella's Cheesehead Lodge."

"I wish I had grown up with a family that did things like this," Maisey says.

"Do you still have family?" I know her parents passed

but maybe she has extended family. Do her people know she's gone? Are tears being shed for Maisey? Is there anyone in her family that might want to take advantage of Maisey? Someone I should have on my radar?

"Not really," she says. "There are a few distant aunts and uncles in Europe, but I was an only child. My folks died when I was in my late teens. Dad had a heart attack and mom passed away from a mystery ailment a year later."

"I'm sorry."

"Me too. Your family looks nice," she says. "Tell me about them."

"Great Aunt Stella is the short one with the pink hair wearing reindeer antlers."

"She looks hilarious," Maisey says.

"She's the life of every party. Stella owns The Cheesehead Lodge in Two Sisters Bay, Wisconsin."

"It looks magical," she says. "I wish I had visited The Cheesehead before, well ..."

"It is magical." I spot Theodore staring at the seaweed on her shoe and my stomach flip-flops because I'm scared he's going to try and nibble on that stuff again.

"Tell me more," she says.

Maisey's interesting and fun in a dangerous kind of way. If we were in high school, she'd have taught me how to shoplift. We would have played hooky and hung out with cute boys who drove fast, flashy cars. We would have gone to parties held by the cool kids and made out with football players on the Varsity team.

But the longer Maisey lives at my place, the more my cat is capable of seeing ghosts. Unless I decide to sell him to a local psychic, or pop for his kitty shrink bills, this isn't going to get either of us anywhere.

I need to figure out what happened to Maisey and I need to do so quickly. I hoist Theodore up and scratch his ears. "Let's talk about them later. I need to be at work in an hour."

"You have a day job?"

"Absolutely. It's a part-time gig." I walk toward my bedroom.

"More ghostly business?" She follows me.

"No." I deposit my cat on the floor and he skitters off with a few weird hops.

"Something else supernatural?" Maisey asks. "Do you read tarot cards? Hold Ouija board séances? Dabble in witchy things? I could teach you how to cleanse auras if you want."

"No, thanks. I'm good." I grab clothes from my closet and toss them on the bed. "I leave the witchy things to Great Aunt Stella and my cousin Izzy. You might think my family looks normal, but scratch the surface and they have all kinds of weirdo habits."

"Like what?"

I pull on black pants and a long-sleeved cotton V-neck top. "Uncle Elliot is an inventor."

"Cool."

"Not really," I say. "Some of his inventions are real. Some are imaginary. Izzy is taking Zoom classes to become a witch. And you can count your blessings that you never attended one of Stella's pot-luck Ouija board séances."

"I'd love to attend a pot-luck séance."

"Too many carbs and too much booze," I say. "I have a practical job. I'm a baker for Mort Feinberg."

"The man who owns Feinberg's Famous Deli?"

"Yes. I've been working for him for almost three years now."

"That's the best deli in Beverly Hills."

"Right? I work a few half-days every week. Pound out whatever he needs for the restaurant and private parties."

"Not a bad gig,"

"I love it." I pause in front of the mirror, and open my makeup bag.

"Why don't I come with you?" she asks.

"Not a good idea," I say. "This is actual work. No time to chit chat."

"I'll hang out."

"Can't do that either." I swipe on blush and mascara. "I'll be busy baking chocolate babka and rugelach."

"But I can give you advice."

"I don't need advice."

"Everyone needs advice," she says.

"Not me."

"Especially you."

I glare at her. "Like what?"

"You need…" She stares at me and narrows her eyes. "You need more mascara."

"I do?" I glance in the mirror.

"Yes. Never skimp on mascara. "

I pick up the wand and add another layer. You're right."

"See? Good advice. Please, let me come with you, I won't bother you a bit. I'll wander around Beverly Hills and window shop. When you're done, we can hunt down more clues."

I do the other eye.

"Bonus, Elaine's cousin, David Davenport, the money skimmer, works nearby," she says.

"How do you know?" I make my way to the living room.

"His address was on the snail mail he sent Mason," she says. "325 Roxbury Drive, Beverly Hills."

"You've got a good memory." I grab a coat from the rack.

"It used to be good. After I passed, I could barely remember a thing about what happened to me the night of Mason's party. But now, I think it's coming back."

"That's great." I shrug on my jacket and eye the bruise on her shoulder. It's purple and blue and red. If I squint, it almost looks like the imprint of a hand. "What do you remember?"

"I was in the kitchen at the Malibu house grabbing a drink. Frankie and I started talking. I told her I hated Elaine. She told me Elaine might not be in the picture for much longer. She and Mason were thinking about getting back together."

"Oh. How did you feel about that?"

"I think..." She frowns, her forehead knitting. "I think my hands went numb."

"That's shock." My heart squeezes in sympathy. I am no stranger to shock and it always sucks.

"I could deal with 'placeholder' Elaine. I knew I could win Mason back from her. It was only a matter of time. But Frankie?"

Goosebumps prickle on the back of my neck. "Yes?"

"I couldn't compete with Frankie. I *wouldn't* compete with Frankie. I like her. She's smart and funny and talented. Mason would be lucky to date her again. I had to let go of my dream of getting back with him." She sniffles.

"What did you do? Did you leave the party?"

She nods. "I did. I walked all the way to the end of that street. The one where you parked your car. And I cried."

"I'm sorry." I'm sniffling now, too.

"I climbed the sand dunes and made my way out to the ocean. I didn't want anyone from the party to see me lose it. I walked away from Mason's house until the sand ended at the boulders. I wanted to go around them. I tried to go around them. I waded into the water, but suddenly I was in the ocean up to my knees. The surf grew rougher and I couldn't go any farther. I had to let it go."

Her memories really are coming back. "And?"

"That's it." She scrunches her face. "That's all I remember."

Mascara will forever splotch her pretty face. The seaweed on her shoe will always drip. Her bruised shoulder and the crazy blonde wig will always make her look like a beat-up doll that was rough-housed and then coldly discarded.

My throat tightens. "I changed my mind. Come with me to Feinberg's Deli. Wander Beverly Hills. Window shop. Who doesn't like window shopping on Rodeo Drive?"

"OK." She wipes away her tears.

"We'll meet up after my shift and investigate a clue or two. What do you think?"

"Sounds good." We walk to my car. "Maybe I can practice my new poltergeist skills."

"On Rodeo Drive?"

She nods.

"No, you shouldn't practice your poltergeist skills on Rodeo Drive." I start laughing. "No, *really,* you shouldn't."

Then we both laugh.

❧

MAISEY'S OUT tooling around Beverly Hills when Mort Feinberg toddles into the recently updated stainless steel kitchen at his kitschy, charming deli. "Graceland, what are you working on?"

"Chocolate babka, sir."

I first met Mort a few years back when we shared an elevator during a visit to our respective doctors' offices. We struck up a conversation. He gave me a job after my baking business tanked when I briefly became a suspect in the murder of Dr. Derrick Fuller, the obnoxious, self-help author. I kept working for Mort thereafter because he was the best boss in the world, and who doesn't love a regular pay check?

"Is this a good batch?" Mort stares at the pastries cooling on racks. He's a sweetheart, somewhere between eighty and ageless. He's five feet two inches on a good day, and a mess of wrinkles and blue eyes that twinkle behind thick, black-framed glasses. Today he wears pants belted high on his waist, a pastel blue shirt neatly tucked in, and thick shoes.

I take a tray of piping hot pastries from the oven. "They're delicious." I cut him a sample from an already cooled dessert, place it on a little plate, and hand it to him along with a fork.

He takes a bite and hums a little under his breath. "This is a good batch."

"Agree," I say. "Just like you ordered."

"You've got company. Someone's waiting for you in the front."

"Really?" I glance up at the clock. Ten minutes to go until quitting time. Who would be waiting for me other than Maisey? I hope Mort can't see her.

"A man," Mort says. "Forty-something with good posture. I wish I had paid more attention to my posture when I was his age." He stands a little straighter and sucks in his stomach.

"Did you catch a name?"

"Nope. You know, half the time I don't hear what people are saying anymore. I pretend like I do, but I don't. I'm taking a class on lip reading but I'm not that good at it yet."

"None of us are perfect, sir," I say a little louder, a little slower, and point to the pastry. "Want another piece?"

"Yes."

I cut him a chunk and put it on his plate.

He dives into it. "Best decision I ever made was hiring you."

"Best opportunity I've ever been offered," I say, and we share a smile.

Chapter 15

MY MYSTERY VISITOR

Pete's my mystery visitor. He's sitting in a red leather booth at the back of the joint. "Good afternoon," I say. "How'd you find me?"

"You left Mort Feinberg as a reference on your job application for Mason's party." His face is etched with sadness. His clothes are rumpled, a ketchup stain on the edge of his shirt. He looks worse than Mason looked a few days ago at Frankie's art show.

"Right."

"You have a minute?" He gestures to the seat across from him.

"Sure," I say, and settle in. "What's up?"

He removes an envelope from his coat pocket. "Firstly, Mason wanted me to give you this."

I take it from him, open it, and give it a scan. It's a contract. "Wow," I say. "This is more than generous."

Maisey materializes. "I'll say." She sneaks a peek at the contract for another catering gig and scooches into the booth next to me. "Move over, please."

I do, all the while staring at the paper Pete has just handed me. It's a work for hire agreement for a "Memorial for Maisey" party Mason's hosting. Once again, he wants me to bake the desserts and serve them at the event.

The date's just a few days away, a week to the day that Maisey passed. The crowd will be a little smaller. He's invited around fifty of Maisey's nearest and dearest. "This is a lot of money," I say.

"It's last minute." Pete sips his coffee. "Mason believes in your talent and appreciates your work. He knows the desserts will be in capable hands."

"Isn't it a little early for a celebration of life?"

"That's what I thought. Mason reminded me that a lot of people who came into town for his birthday are still in L.A. Unless he hosts a Zoom service, it's going to be easier to memorialize Maisey now rather than later."

"Good point," Maisey says.

A barely nibbled corned beef and Swiss cheese sandwich sits on a plate in front of Pete.

"You don't like the sandwich?" I realize I sound just like my mother, and I cringe a little.

"Not hungry," he says.

"He looks like crap," Maisey says. "He's a big guy and works out a lot. He needs the calories. He needs to eat that."

"Why?" I ask.

"Losing someone I care about does that to me," he says.

Maisey blinks.

"Losing a friend is tough." Elaine and Frankie mentioned that Pete and Maisey had dated in the past. A sweet vibe lingers between them. "Not eating isn't going to bring her back. Besides, Feinberg's makes the best Reuben in Los Angeles. Work it off at the gym."

"Once I get back there," he says.

"What does that mean?" Maisey frowns. "He's ex-military. His workouts are as regular as sunrise."

"Eat," I say, and point at his sandwich. "Or I will."

He takes a bite. Then another.

I re-read the contract. "Mason's party for Maisey is this Friday, 7 p.m. at Mason's Marina del Rey house."

He nods. "You've been there. I drove you when he was late for your interview at Moto Gear last week."

"Right. It's a pretty place." It's hard to believe it's only been a week since I was interviewed to cater for his birthday party. The home was tucked behind upscale condos and five- star hotels on the peninsula's beach. It's a perfect example of one of the things I love the most about Los Angeles: little pockets of Zen are sprinkled throughout the city.

"Out of all of Mason's houses, that's my favorite," Maisey says. "It's so peaceful and yet close to the best Venice restaurants."

"I'm partial to that place," Pete says. "It's smack dab on the beach with views of the wetlands. Yet you can watch the planes as they take off from LAX and fly out over the Pacific."

"Dolphins swim close to the breakwater in the late afternoon," Maisey says. "Pete's the one that showed them to me for the first time. It was magical."

I perk up. "Really?"

She nods and extends a tentative hand across the table toward his plate.

"Really." Pete looks up from the few bites left of his sandwich. He reaches for the potato chips and brushes fingers with Maisey as they grasp the same cluster. They freeze, and curious looks play off their faces. My breath catches.

"What?" Pete asks.

"Finish your sandwich. You still have a couple of bites left."

"I'm hankering for a chip," he says, not letting go of the one both he and Maisey are holding.

"I practiced my new poltergeist skills at a little boutique on Rodeo Drive today." Maisey wears a determined look and squeezes that chip just a little harder.

Oh no.

Sister Cecelia takes a seat at the four-top across the aisle from us. *"You do not want a kerfuffle between a newly minted poltergeist and her ex-boyfriend in the middle of Mort's deli."* She's dressed a little nicer for Beverly Hills, wearing a below the knee black skirt paired with a soft blush-colored cardigan, and a strand of fat pearls. Her hair is neatly combed and secured with a headband.

"What should I do?"

"When in doubt," she says scanning a menu, *"distract."*

"Pete." I slip the contract back in the envelope and slide it inside my purse. "I'll get back to you."

"Sounds good." Pete doesn't move a muscle, and continues staring at the chips.

"A female clerk at the boutique was ignoring a woman," Maisey says. "I think she was a tourist. She was dressed in a Chicago Bears football jersey and leggings. She asked about trying on some clothes but the shopkeeper pretended not to notice her."

"It's like watching a high stakes chess game." My gaze flips between the two of them. *"Should I do something?"*

"Yes," Sister Cecelia says. *"Pacify the poltergeist."*

"How?"

"Figure it out. How are the Reubens here?"

"Great."

"Did I tell you I despise pretentious people who lie?" Maisey asks.

Oh God, I hope Maisey doesn't try to throw something at Pete. Even more importantly, I hope Mort isn't around to witness poltergeist phenomena. As sturdy as he looks, he had a heart attack a few years back, and I'm not sure his ticker could take it. I break into a sweat and fan my face.

"The clerk said the dressing rooms were all filled up. I looked. They weren't," Maisey says. "They were just closed from the inside. I unlatched the doors and pushed them open. It wasn't that hard, really. It could have been a gust of wind that blew through the shop."

Maisey yanks on the chip. It flies off Pete's plate and lands on the table between them. She concentrates, frown lines furrowing between her brows as she drags the potato chip toward her.

Pete stares as it slip-slides across the table, his eyes widening. "What the..."

I snap my fingers. "*When* do you need a reply?"

"About?" He blinks.

"The chip. I mean Mason's contract."

"Tonight."

"Tonight, it is. Sorry to cut this short, but there's someplace I'm supposed to be. People I need to see. Things I need to... I need to go!" I elbow Maisey in the ribs.

"Oof. Fine." She breaks her death stare with the potato chip and scoots out of the booth. She glares at Pete, then turns and strides toward the deli's front door.

I stand and grab his tab. "Sandwich is on me. Great to see you."

"Annie," Pete says.

"What?"

"Did you hang out with Maisey?"

"What do you mean?" My cheeks grow warm.

"You know. After you met her at Moto Gear."

I hesitate. "Yes."

"So, then you know," he says, picking up the stray potato chip lying alone and forlorn in the middle of the table.

"Know what?" I ask.

"That Maisey's magical."

"Yes." I say and watch as he pops the chip in his mouth. "Yes, I do."

❧

"YOU CAN'T JUST CALL big shot money managers and get an appointment at the last minute," I say as Maisey and I walk the few blocks toward my car. I normally get off work at the deli in time to miss the worst of the traffic. But talking with Pete set me back about a half hour, which can add an hour and half to my commute home.

"Just do it," Maisey says. "If I weren't dead and saddled with you, I would have done it already."

"Saddled?" I pluck my phone from my purse and call David Davenport's office. "Says the recently departed woman who moved into my place and commandeered my bedroom."

"Put it on speaker," Maisey says.

I click the phone's button.

"Davenport Investments. How might I direct your call?"

"I'd love to set up an appointment with Mr. Davenport," I say. "I know it's spur of the moment, but I'm in Beverly Hills this afternoon."

"That's nice. Mr. Davenport's booked for a few weeks. Can I take your name and number and message you back with some available times next month?"

"Um," I say. "Okay."

"Tell him you're friends with Mason Callaway," Maisey says.

"I'm friends with Mason Callaway," I say, and cross my fingers.

"Aha," the assistant says. "Mr. Davenport has a sliver of time today at 4:45. Shall I save that slot?"

"Yes, thank you." I give him my name and click off.

We pass trendy restaurants, chic boutiques, and pristine brown brick professional buildings on our way to David's office "What's the plan of attack?" Maisey asks.

"I don't know. This was your idea. I thought I'd wing it."

She frowns. "Wing it?"

I stare up at the addresses on the buildings. This is the one. It's a pretty, brown brick, five-story building with a directory. I lean in, scan the names, find the code, and punch it in. Seconds later we are buzzed in at exactly 4:30 p.m., and directed to wait in the small antechamber.

Maisey plunks down on a chair and sprawls out. "I'm sleepy."

"Shopping does that to me too," I say.

She yawns. "Going to take a little nap. Wake me when things get exciting."

"K."

Dog-eared magazines lie on a side table. I thumb through a few, check my watch, and notice that 4:45 p.m. has come and gone. I crack my neck, stand, and check out the cheap art and other pictures on the walls.

Amidst the mess of mediocrity is one photo of inter-est: a framed eight by ten photo of David surrounded by a cluster of happy middle school kids wearing soccer uniforms emblazoned with fat bees. I lean in and read the plaque underneath. "David Davenport: Club Bumblebees' Person of the Year!"

Maisey opens her eyes and stretches her arms over her head. "I'm bored. Is this guy ever going to show up?"

The assistant's hunched over and scrolling on his phone.

"Hi there," I say. "Is Mr. Davenport— "

"David will be here soon," he says.

Maisey stands. "I'm going to check out his office."

"Maybe that's not such a good idea," I whisper.

She ignores me, walks past the assistant, and enters the glassed-in cubicle.

I sit back down and flip through a worn *People Magazine Sexiest Man Alive* issue from a few years back. I wonder how in the hell Davenport can do business like this, let alone manage the money of multi-millionaire Mason Callaway.

The door leading from the office complex's hallway to the antechamber opens with a squeak. "Sorry I'm late." David enters and extends his hand. "Ms. Graceland?"

"Yes." I shake his hand.

"Come with me." He strides past his assistant. "You can leave, Lionel."

"Yes, sir. I left that file you wanted on your desk."

I follow David into his glassed-in space.

"Give me just one quick minute," he says.

Maisey walks away from his ergonomic chair seconds before David plunks down in it. He peruses the folder.

"I checked all the scribbles on his desk calendar," Maisey says, eyeing the floor-to-ceiling bookcase. "I read every scrap of paper in his trashcan that wasn't stuck to a piece of gum. This guy has a serious chewing gum problem."

"Gum?" I say.

"Sure." David slides a pack across the desk toward me.

"Oh, thank you." I hesitantly take a stick.

"There are wads of icky, old balled up gum stuck in that basket," Maisey continues. "His cleaning crew does not do a good job. They're probably budget, just like this office."

I drop the stick back on the desk.

"Not your flavor?" David asks.

"I gave it up for Lent."

Maisey points to a framed photo of David on a bookshelf, surrounded by gorgeous, smiling children wearing soccer uniforms. "See this picture?" she says. It's almost identical to the one in the waiting room."

I nod.

"This is the charity *I* support," she says. "I was Club Bumblebees' person of the year a while back. How weird is that?"

"How do you know Mason Callaway?" David asks.

"I've done some work for him," I say.

"That makes two of us." He doesn't look up from the file.

Maisey peers at the open file. "I haven't seen one piece of paper with Mason's name on it," she says. "Nothing with his address. Nothing that indicates what he's investing in. I tried to open the drawers but they're locked. I can't break into his computer. This is a total waste of time. Let's go."

David closes the file on his desk with a smack. "You've come to the right place. It's never too early or late for that matter to start investing."

I see the name on the tab the same time Maisey does. "MILLER, MAISEY."

❈ 16 ❈

Chapter 16

NOT a PURITAN

❧

"What the hell is David Davenport doing with a file on me?" Maisey goes to grab the folder but only manages to push it off the desk. It lands on the floor with a clop. Papers scatter.

"Huh?" David says. "That's weird."

Maisey's hands are trembling. "I've never done business with this guy," she says. "Why does he have a file on me?"

"I don't know." All the little hairs on the back of my neck prickle.

"You don't know what?" David asks.

"Why I gave up gum for Lent," I say. "What was I thinking?"

Maisey's face turns as green as the seaweed dripping off her shoe "I don't feel so good."

I bend down to pick up papers. "Everything's going to be all right."

"Of course it is." He rises from his chair.

"I can pick those up for you," I say.

"Even better. Take some of those papers," Sister Cecelia whispers.

"That's stealing," I silently say.

"You're a murderologist," she says. *"Not a Puritan."*

I cram a few papers in my purse and distract David by tossing others on the desk.

He is up and out of his chair.

"I want to hit him," Maisey says.

A chill runs down my spine because the look on her face is serious. "Don't."

She picks up the pack of gum. If I squint, it looks like it's levitating.

"Oh my God," David freezes.

"Drop it," I say.

"Fine." Maisey hurls the pack. It flies a few feet through the air and bounces off David's chin.

"Ack!" He scrambles behind his ergonomic chair.

"Uh-oh. Did we just have a mild quake?" I stand, clutch my purse tight to my body, and stride toward the door. "Oops. Look at the time. I didn't realize it was so late."

"Who *are* you?"

"Annie Graceland," I say. "Dessert baker. Lovely to meet you. Gotta run."

I hustle down the hallway and hit the elevator button. If I'm lucky I'll be in my car and headed toward Venice before he realizes half his file on Maisey is missing.

MAISEY PACES in my living room. Her blonde wig shivers with every anxious step. Theodore tries to rub up against her ankles but after she stumbles over him, he skedaddles. "I can't believe it's come to this."

"What do you mean?" She's so upset and I don't know how to calm her down.

"A week ago, I was meeting a friend at Moto Gear. We were going to talk about books and writing, gossip and parties. But then I tripped over David Davenport and I landed on you."

"I know."

"I feel horrible about that, I really do. I flattened your desserts and I almost messed up your interview with Mason."

"I got the job." I sit in my chair at my desk.

"A couple of days later I'm dead. I'm pretty sure someone killed me although I don't know who, and you're the only person who can hear me."

I rack my brain, wondering if I can get her anything, think of anything, that will calm her down.

"You can't," Sister Cecelia says. She sits in my purple overstuffed armchair in front of the fireplace doing a crossword puzzle.

"I feel so helpless," I say, scrunching my fists. *"I want to help."*

"You are. You're listening. Perhaps that's the most important thing right now."

Maisey wipes a few tears away, and jams her fists on her waist. "And I know that you're trying to figure out who killed me. I know that you're investigating, but I'm frustrated, and feeling angrier. And today I find out that the creep who might be stealing from Mason has a file with my name on it? Why? I feel more violated, if that's even possible."

"I'm so sorry." I bite my lip. "Do you have any idea why he'd have the file?"

"I don't." She shrugs. "Figure it out, murderologist. You're the one with experience in this kind of thing. Not me."

&

I STAY up half the night going through the papers I swiped from David's office. There are a few problems. The papers I crammed in my bag have no page numbers. The wrinkled sheets are primarily filled with indecipherable lines annotated with dates, dollar amounts, and what look like code words. "What does this mean?" I mumble and stare at a few entries.

June 15, 20XX Bookmobile $20,000.00

March 7, 20XX Bumblebees $30,000.00

My head feels like its spinning as I try to make sense of this gobbledygook. At 3 a.m. I throw my hands up in the air. "I can't do this. It's indecipherable."

"You're just tired," Sister Cecelia says. She rests on my purple over-stuffed chair, sipping a cup of tea. She wears a blue fluffy robe and matching fat, fleecy slippers. *"Get some sleep. Look at them in the morning with fresh eyes. You'll figure it out."*

"I tell myself that every day since this terrible thing happened." I sigh and lean back in my ergonomic chair. *"I*

don't know who killed Maisey. I'm not even sure I have a prime suspect."

"What does your gut tell you?"

"I don't like Tina or Heidi."

"Mason's ex-girlfriends?"

"Yes. And supposedly Maisey's friends. I've had next to no up close and personal time with them, but from what Maisey tells me they are frosty and two-faced."

"Does that make them killers?"

"I don't know."

"Who else?"

"Whoever had access to Maisey when she wandered out of Mason's house at the party?" I stand, stretching my arms over my head.

"Who was that?"

"I never saw Frankie the entire night." I walk to the couch and toss the pillows onto the wood floor. "Maisey said she followed her outside to the dunes. They shared a few puffs of weed."

"What would Frankie's motive be?"

"I don't have a clue." I unfold the fold-out couch, opening it with a creak. "I met her at the art show and she seemed normal."

"Who else?"

"Elaine disappeared for around half an hour before the birthday cake was rolled out."

"Her motive?"

"Ugh. Too much to count. She's a weird one." I pluck the blue quilted Afghan off the couch and toss it onto the sofa bed. I fluff the pillows. "I don't want to think about that or I won't fall asleep."

"Why did the money manager have a file with Maisey's name on it? Did she do business with him?"

"You really *don't want me to sleep tonight, do you?"* I glance at my desk. The papers with Maisey's name stamped on top are in plain sight. *"Maisey claims she didn't."*

"Then why does he have dollar signs inked on paper pages?"

"And we're back at square one because I don't know." I tap the papers into a neat stack and slide them into a drawer. I don't want Maisey stumbling upon them in the middle of the night when she's restless and roaming the apartment.

"Where does this leave you?" Sister Cecelia asks.

"There's no reason for David Davenport to have a file on her." I head to the kitchen and brush my teeth at the sink.

"Why's your toothbrush in here?"

"That's not part of the current mystery." I spit into the sink and run the water.

"And yet I'm still curious."

"Because I don't want Maisey playing poltergeist with it."

"Got it. Tell me about David."

"He's Elaine's cousin and Mason Callaway's money manager." I pad back into the living room, pick up Theodore, and cradle him. *"And he's a notorious man spreader."*

"Anything else?"

My cat squeaks in protest but I scratch his chin and he goes quiet. *"Maisey thinks he was skimming funds from Mason."*

"Skimming funds. A file with Maisey's name on it. Dollar amounts on the pages. That's a good clue."

"I think you're right," I say, and crawl into bed.

"Sleep tight, murderologist," Sister Cecelia says. *"You're on the right track."*

THURSDAYS ARE USUALLY my days off. I do a little house-cleaning, laundry, and schedule some self-care — like a Chinese foot massage or a chiropractic visit. Sometimes I take in an early matinee when a movie's been out for a while and I know there'll be almost no one there.

But there is no rest for the wicked this Thursday, as I'm baking a new batch of desserts for Maisey's memorial tomorrow.

The 'ghost' of honor has left my apartment for parts unknown. "Don't forget tomorrow is your big party," I said, and immediately felt like an idiot.

"Do you think I have time to do my hair?" she asked, patting her wig.

"I...I..."

She laughed and dematerialized in front of my face.

I selected one of my many baking playlists. My current favorite features songs from Kate Bush, Beyoncé, and Taylor Swift. I spread out the ingredients on the kitchen counter to the left of the sink. The large stand mixer is plugged in on the right.

For Mason's birthday party, I went with mini-cheese-cakes, chocolate cupcakes, and mixed berry tarts.

I'm changing it up for Maisey's memorial. I flipped through my big book of yummy recipes. I picked pumpkin cupcakes slathered in cream cheese frosting, bourbon apple cinnamon tarts with a crumble topping, and my grandmother's cannoli recipe.

I'm mixing ingredients when my phone rings. I glance at the screen. Great Aunt Stella. I turn off the mixer and pick up.

"Annie?" she asks.

"Auntie Stella. Are you okay?" She's in her mid-eighties, is in decent health, but I never want to tempt fate.

"I'm fine, honey. You are never going to believe what your mother said to me the other day."

"I bet you're right." Half the time I can't believe what my mother says to *me*. This is a popular topic of conversation between us. "But I can't talk about that right now."

"It'll just take a minute," she says.

"Seriously, my favorite auntie in the whole world, I've got a big bowl full of dough and dozens of desserts to bake for a gig tomorrow."

"I'm you're only auntie."

I smile. "I know. Can I have a raincheck? I'll call you this weekend."

"Absolutely, my darling. Remind me to tell you about the new ghost I spotted in the hallway on the third floor at The Cheesehead."

"A new one, eh?" Aunt Stella owns the haunted Cheesehead Lodge in Two Sisters Bay, Wisconsin. A new ghost spotting is always cause for excitement. "I can't wait to hear all about it. Love you."

"Love you back."

An hour or so later I pull the first batch of apple tarts from the oven. There's a knock on my living room door. "Who is it?" I holler, but I can see it's already opening with a squeak.

"Not Santa," Julia says, and shuts it with a clunk. "How come you're not returning my texts?"

"What texts?"

She makes her way into the kitchen and drops her purse on the table. "The ones I sent this morning."

"My phone's probably on mute."

"Maisey here?" She looks around.

"Nope."

"Where is she? Hunting down clues?"

"Do I look like Maisey's keeper?"

"Nope. It smells delicious in here. How goes the investigation?" She hovers over the pan of tarts cooling on a tray and inhales.

"Slow." I finish pouring the cupcake batter into the non-stick muffin tin and pop it in the oven.

"Anything I can help you with?"

"Not with the mystery about who killed her, but you can be my taste tester," I say.

"I like that better." She swipes a napkin from the holder, removes a tart with a spatula, and bites into it. "Yum. What's the event you're baking for?"

"Maisey's memorial." I pull a batch of cannoli from the oven. "It's tomorrow."

"Did I know about this?"

"I don't think so. It's happening quickly. Mason wants to do a little something before all the out-of-town guests leave. Want to be my assistant?"

Chapter 17

AN INTERPRETER

"Jeez, I don't know," Julia says. "The birthday party last week was so much fun."

"You don't have to."

"Nah. Count me in." She pulls her tablet out of her purse. "But first, I need your help."

"With?"

"Picking the last few photos for my website. Can you take a mini- break?"

"Yes." I check the timer. I've got five minutes left on a batch of cupcakes. "Coffee?"

"Please." She takes a seat. "I've combed through five thousand photos. I've already bought about twenty but I have a niche I still need to fill out."

"What do you mean, a niche?" I set the coffee mugs on the table and take a seat across from her.

"I need to target people who like kids," she says, scrolling on her tablet.

"Kids?" I scooch my chair a little closer.

"Yes. I need visuals to cover family law. Pictures that imply I like children. Photos that telegraph my boutique law practice is family friendly."

"Got it," I say, staring at her tablet.

"I narrowed down my favorites." She clicks on a folder and curated images pop up bright as an assortment of jelly beans. "I want your opinion. Vote yes or no on the one I point to and tell me why. Okay?"

"K.".

She taps a photo. "This one."

"No on the pre-pubescent kid with the red bozo hair and painted face dressed in a clown suit terrorizing his friends."

"Why?"

"He has an early moustache and people are scared of clowns. You don't want to imply you are the scary clown lawyer."

"Got it. Deleted. Next." She taps another photo.

"I like this one."

"Why?"

"The smiling mother's painting a house while the little boy and girl help her. It makes me think of home and family."

"Good call." She pulls up another.

"I vote yes on the sexy grandpa and kids playing with the puppy."

"I thought that was cute too." She clicks again.

"What's this?" I ask.

"Kids jumping off a cliff into a swimming hole?"

I squint at the stock photo and tap the screen. "No. This one."

"The middle-graders dressed in soccer uniforms? I thought a 'children playing sports' shot might be appealing."

Maisey materializes next to us and I startle.

"I agree," Maisey says.

"What?" Julia asks, after seeing me jump. "Oh, right. Maisey's here."

"You can't go wrong with pictures of kids playing team sports," Maisey says. "I supported a few children's sports charities. Have I missed anything?"

"Nope," I say and return to the task at hand. "The desserts are coming along. Julia's going to help me tomorrow at your memorial. I think we're good."

"Tell her thanks for helping," Maisey says. "That's sweet of her."

"Maisey says thanks for helping tomorrow."

"My pleasure," Julia says. "I think we got off on the wrong foot after the curtain fire thing."

"We're good. Maisey says. "Do I get a vote?"

"On what?" I ask.

"The photo with the kids in uniform."

I turn to Julia. "Maisey wants to know if she gets to vote on your pictures."

"Why not?" she says.

"There's something weird about that photo," Maisey says.

"Which one?" The oven timer beeps. I jump up and grab a potholder.

"Seriously," Maisey says. "There's something off with that picture."

"We'll figure it out after your memorial," I say, pulling a tray from the oven and then slipping another one in.

Julia closes the lid on her tablet.

"But—" Maisey says.

"I don't want to mess up the desserts. I want them as perfect as possible. It's your party, after all."

ON FRIDAY AFTERNOON, I drive Julia, Maisey, and a batch of freshly-baked desserts to Mason's house. Maisey and Julia yack and I serve as the interpreter between the smart, funny, girl ghost and my smart, funny, BFF.

I vaguely remember the route from when Pete chauffeured me to my job interview a little over a week ago, but after I drive in the wrong direction on Washington Boulevard, I ask Siri for help.

I turn right when the road dead ends at the water channel that connects to the Santa Monica Bay. I turn again, and motor down the narrow street, avoiding a clueless skateboarder and a guy walking his dog. I count the numbers on the houses until I find Mason's place.

"You are here," Siri announces.

"Siri's so smart," I say.

"Not as smart as she thinks she is," Julia says.

I pull into the driveway. A few catering vans are already parked close to the double garage, one door wide open. I pop the hatch and Julia hops out the passenger seat. "Do you want me to unload?"

"Nah, I got it. Go set up. We're in the back yard. This

time I don't have to park a mile away. I'm allowed to stay here for the duration."

"Probably because parking sucks in the Marina," she says, and follows a handful of service people entering through a side gate.

Maisey brushes off her clothes. I suspect it's simply habit because that clump of seaweed dripping off her shoe hasn't changed in a week. "How do I look?" she asks.

"Like you are ready for your big celebration of life."

"It's a small memorial, but thanks for trying to cheer me up." She trails after Julia.

I watch her go and out of nowhere feel choked up. I've been so busy mixing, baking, frosting, and wrapping up all the sweets, I haven't really thought about the meaning of today. It's not just an average party. It's a celebration of life, but Maisey's too young to be earning this distinction.

We should be celebrating another of her milestones. A party for when her next book published, or a birthday, or when she falls in love with someone who's not as flaky as Mason. Someone who will stick around for a while. Someone who might be a forever love.

"Hey." Pete walks out of the garage. "Need help?"

"Can you score me an extra cart?" I ask.

"Sure." A minute later he's rolling one toward me. "I'll help you unload."

"Sounds good." I lift boxes from the back and pass them to him.

He piles them on the trolley. "So, I've been thinking."

"About what?" I ask.

"The other day at the deli."

"What about it?"

"What was up with the levitating potato chip?"

I feel my cheeks burn. "I have no idea what you're talking about."

"I think you do." He leans closer. "I've been making a few inquiries. Remember Dr. Derrick Fuller?"

"Vaguely." I shut the hatchback feeling my stomach drop into my shoes.

"It turns out he wasn't the only murder victim you were associated with. Your name was mentioned in yet another murder."

"Oh, the crazy things you can find on the internet." I place a firm hand on top of the boxes and push the cart through the side entrance. I'm hoping that the wheels rattling on the terra cotta pavers will drown out the sound of my heart banging inside my chest. My fears were materializing.

Pete did indeed notice Maisey's poltergeist shenanigans. Now Mr. ex-military is going to want an explanation, and how in the heck can I explain a levitating potato chip?

"Yes," he says. "A murder at a beauty contest pageant in Wisconsin."

"That was the inaugural Wisconsin's Hometown Guys' contest," I say. "That was tragic. I might have been a pageant judge, but none of what happened was my fault, and the bad guys were brought to justice."

"That's what I read," he says. "Did you know Maisey wrote a book called *The Urban Witch?*"

"Of course. She told me."

"She loved new age-y stuff. She fully embraced a wide range of hocus-pocus."

"That's nice." I don't have time to discuss hocus pocus

because the party's starting. Pop music plays from invisible speakers. Tina, Heidi, and Frankie sip glasses of wine on the deck above us. More people join them. Ghostly shenanigans involving levitating potato chips are not my concern right now.

"I went on some of those gossipy information sites," Pete says. "Dove down that rabbit hole. I read rumors you are a ghost whisperer."

"That's silly," I say. "Do I look like I'm into new-agey stuff?"

"Yes."

"Well, I'm not. I couldn't see an aura if one dove off that palm tree and smacked me on the head."

Julia's at a table in the backyard fussing with a floral arrangement. She looks up and beckons. "Hurry up."

I push the cart a little faster. "Let's talk about this later."

"Did you know Maisey was writing the sequel to *The Urban Witch*," Pete says, his muscular shoulders hiking to his ears.

"Yes."

"Did she tell you the title?"

"No."

"*The Urban Poltergeist*."

I start coughing and I can't stop.

"So you see how it's more than just a little suspicious that Maisey passed away, potato chips are levitating, and you're involved."

"I, I, I..." Goosebumps prickle on the backs of my arms. I don't know what to tell this guy.

Sister Cecelia pipes up. She's dressed in a navy long-sleeved sweater, full skirt, and clutching her rosary. *"Tell him you're a baker and not a ghost hunter."*

"I'm a baker and not a ghost hunter," I say, straighten my spine, sticking my nose in the air for emphasis.

"I'm on to you, Annie Graceland," Pete says.

"Take a ticket and stand in line."

❧ 18 ❧

Chapter 18

THE GUEST of HONOR

❧

Pete and I glare at each other. He breaks the look first. "I don't really talk about it, but I used to care about Maisey. A lot."

My heart squeezes because I've been suspecting this for a while. "I'm sorry for your loss."

"I am too." He stalks off through the growing crowd.

"Thanks," I say to Sister Cecelia.

"Welcome. I get a weird feeling about tonight's gig," she says. *"I think you should be on the lookout."*

"For what?" I roll the cart toward the dessert table.

"You'll know when it happens. Just remember: Lemonade from lemons, murderologist. Everything happens for a reason."

"I always hated that saying."

"Me too." She turns and walks away.

I pull up next to the dessert table. Julia's already arranged the plates, napkins and flowers. "Sorry it took me so long."

"About time." She grabs boxes and flips open the lids. We place the sweets on pretty glass baking carousels and festive platters. It's not a moment too soon, because people are already gravitating toward the dessert table like trick or treating kids high on sugar looking for more candy.

The sun sinks on the horizon over the ocean. Sometimes I forget it's still February. Los Angeles can be season-less. The Marina house has a smaller back yard than Mason's Malibu home. I take a minute to take a breather and survey Maisey's celebration of life party.

There's a bar in one corner with folks clustering around it. A server lights the stone fire pit and it roars to life, flames crackling. I recognize about half the people from Mason's birthday party. Elaine hangs on Mason's arm as he greets small groups of gathered guests. Maisey trails behind them like a lost puppy.

"Do you think the guest of honor is enjoying this?" Julia asks. She opens another box of desserts and replenishes the carousels and half-empty trays.

"I can't tell." I scrape crumbs off the table. "She looks a little overwhelmed."

"I would be too. I'm not even sure how she's doing it. Elaine is horrible. Mason seems kind, but disconnected, almost as if he's checked out. Who else was she close to?"

"Not Tina and Heidi," I say. They're schmoozing with David Davenport next to the bar. "Maybe they need a money manager's advice on how to be first in line at her estate sale to buy her vintage gowns."

"Ugh," Julia says. "What does he want from them?"

"What are you talking about?" I ask.

"He's pulling something out of his wallet and showing it to them. I wonder what it is."

"I don't know. His business card? He's probably trolling for new clients."

Frankie approaches the dessert table. "Annie Graceland, I'm so glad I finally get to try one of your famous desserts."

"Me too. What would you like?" I ask.

"What do you have?"

"Bourbon apple tarts. Pumpkin cupcakes with cream cheese frosting, cannoli made from my Italian grandmother's recipe."

"Ooh," she says. "I can't decide."

"Take one of each," Julia says.

"Too much," Frankie says. "I'd explode."

David Davenport makes his way to her. "I'll split them with you. Besides, I've been meaning to talk with you."

"Perfect," Frankie says.

"Oh, hi, David," Julia says. "Remember me? Julia Devereaux."

"No," he says.

"We hung out a few years ago," she says.

"I don't recall," he says.

Julia grabs the knife from the table but I take it from her and whisper, "No stabbing party guests."

She sighs.

I split an apple tart, put pieces on two plates.

Maisey materializes and shoves a hand on her hip. "What's *he* doing here?"

"Everyone loves desserts," I say and pass the plates to Frankie and David. "Here you go. This will get you started."

"Thank you." Frankie bites into the tart. "David, you're Elaine's cousin, right?"

"And Mason's money manager. I saw you at his birthday party last week. Sorry we didn't have a chance to connect."

I slice a pumpkin cupcake and a cannoli down the middle. I arrange the pieces on two more plates.

Frankie wipes crumbs from her lips with a napkin. "Didn't I meet you at my art show at Vida V gallery?"

"I wanted to make it but I couldn't," David says. "I was helping Elaine's mother organize her investment portfolio and charitable donations."

"That's sweet of you," Frankie says.

"Thank you," he says. Speaking of which, do you have anyone guiding you in today's market? You're a successful artist. You don't want to keep all your earnings in a savings account or low interest investments. It's the perfect time to have someone savvy and honest guide you. Who better to trust than Mason Callaway's money manager?"

"Good point," Frankie says. "But I already have help with my investments."

"I also work with several worthwhile charities," David pulls his wallet from his pocket, slipping a laminated photo from it. "Aren't these kids the cutest? They're an underprivileged youth sports organization. Club Bumble-bees. In fact, Maisey contributed to the Bumblebees. I think it was her favorite charity."

"That's terrific," Frankie says. "I'm happy to make a donation in Maisy's honor."

"Club Bumblebees?" Maisey asks. "I knew I recognized that picture."

"What picture?" I ask.

Maisey points to the dog-eared copy in David's hand. "That's the charity I supported. I was Club Bumblebees' Person of the Year. Those are the kids I helped raise money for."

I flash to the entry in the papers I swiped from David's office. The one that said,

"March 7, 20XX Bumblebees $30,000.00."

What does this *mean*?

"I don't feel so good." Maisey shakes her hands.

And it dawns on me.

"Julia," I say. "Don't you want to make a donation to Maisey's favorite charity? Club Bumblebees. David has a picture."

She stares at me funny.

"Take a look," I say and point.

Dollar signs flash in David's eyes. "Oh, *now* I remember you. Successful attorney – right?" He holds out the photo of the cute kids wearing soccer uniforms.

"That's, that's... a stock photo," Julia says.

"That you bought off a stock photo site," I say. "Those kids aren't real."

"Attention," Mason says. He stands next to the fire pit. The sweet version of *Somewhere Over the Rainbow* plays low in the background through speakers. "Attention, please."

The crowd hushes.

"I want to thank everyone for turning out today for Maisey's memorial. Thanks to those of you who changed travel plans, who carved out time in their busy schedules to show up tonight."

"I have no idea what you're talking about," David says in a low voice. "Frankie, I wish I could stay for the ceremony but I have another engagement." He turns to go.

I latch onto his wrist. "Why do you have file on Maisey Miller? A file with an entry for thirty thousand dollars for a children's charity filled with stock photo children? Children that don't exist? Children that aren't real?"

"Take your hand off me," David says.

"No. We need to talk about this."

We struggle. I clamp down harder.

"I *really* don't feel good," Maisey says, pacing. She runs an anxious hand through her blonde wig.

Mason drones on. "I can tell you with a certainty that when we celebrated my birthday a week ago, I had no idea we'd be together again, celebrating a far greater accomplishment. Maisey's life."

David yanks his hand away. I lose my balance and catch myself on the table, hard, taking out half a tray of desserts.

Frankie gasps.

"Are you all right?" Julia asks.

David strides through the crowd.

"I remember," Maisey says. "Oh, no. I remember."

"Stop that guy!" I holler.

He keeps his head down and walks faster.

The crowd hushes and the attention turns in our direction.

"That's the guy who killed me," Maisey says.

My heart drops because I'm the *only* one who can hear her. "Make him stop, Maisey. You need to *make* him stop."

Maisey looks around, unsure. She picks up a cupcake from the table, cocks her arm, and hurls it at him.

It smacks him in the face. Frosting smears across his eyes. He stumbles.

Pete turns his attention toward me.

"Stop him, Pete," I say. "Please. For Maisey."

Pete tackles him. And that's that.

I am on Malibu beach just yards from where Maisey was murdered. It's a misty afternoon, and more than a hint of rain is in the air. The yellow crime tape has been taken down. You'd never know from looking at this piece of pricey beach real estate scattered with ocean stones and shells that a young woman lost her life here due to one person's greed.

Maisey stands in the wet sand, the wind rustling her blonde wig, watching a barefoot Pete skip stones into the ocean. "Yay! You're so good." She claps her hands and follows his lead.

It will take a crack forensic accountant to comb through Mason Callaway's financials and find where and when and how much David Davenport skimmed from him. But Maisey? David outright stole from her through the fictitious charities that he invented.

"Why do you think he did it?" Sister Cecelia asks. My imaginary pep talk coach sits on the sand next to me. She's once again dressed in golf attire, wearing gloves, and clutching a putter.

"*David Davenport was entitled and cut corners. He didn't know right from wrong,*" I silently say.

"*He couldn't do an honest day's work, and made up for it by stealing from others,*" Sister Cecelia says. "*Maisey probably seemed like an easy mark.*"

"*She might have looked like an airhead, but she was good with details.*"

"*Unfortunately, she was good with* other *people's details.*"

"*Maisey had suspected David had been stealing from Mason,*" I say. "*She had never imagined that he'd been stealing from her.*"

"*How did David latch onto her?*"

"*Elaine referred her to him,*" I say. "*She knew Maisey wanted to do something good with some of the money her parents had left her.*"

"*Was Elaine in on the con?*"

"*I don't think so.*" I shake my head.

"*So, she had spent tens of thousands of dollars funding the Bumblebee's Soccer Club charity for underprivileged children.*"

"*She had also donated money to a Bookmobile that didn't exist,*" I say. "*David had done mock-ups of those fake charities using images he had purchased from photo sites.*"

"*The adorable, underprivileged 'soccer kids' were just stock photos available to download for a few bucks?*"

"*Yup,*" I say. "*But David's all consuming need to be seen as important had been his downfall.*"

"*How so?*" Sister Cecelia asks.

"*He had manipulated his own picture into the stock photo of the cute soccer kids and had hung it on his office wall.*"

"*The same photo he'd included in his charity proposal to Maisey?*"

"*Yes,*" I say. "*The same photo series that Julia had stumbled upon while scrolling stock photo sites.*"

"So many thieves are idiots," Sister Cecelia says.

"At the birthday party, Frankie confided to Maisey that she and Mason had been thinking about getting back together. Maisey got upset. She left the house and wandered out to the beach to cry it out."

"But Frankie was her true friend and followed her. Right?" Sister Cecelia asks.

"Right. They talked some more, had a good cry, and got a little high. Frankie had returned to the house in time for the lighting of the birthday cake, but Maisey had stayed behind to sift through her feelings. Her inhibitions had been lowered when she spotted David walking on the beach and texting. She had decided to confront him about her suspicions that he had been stealing from Mason."

"But he had denied it," Sister Cecelia says.

"A fight ensued. He had shaken her, and she had fallen, hitting her head on a rock," I say. *"He'd left and she'd died. The rest is history."*

"I hope David Davenport rots in hell," Sister Cecelia says.

"Me too."

"Gotta fly, murderologist," Sister Cecelia says. *"I'm sure we'll talk soon."*

"Thanks for all your help," I say.

"You're welcome. See you." And poof! She is gone.

"Hey Pete," I say. "I need to talk to Maisey. It's time."

"Okay," he says. "I'll wait for you in the car." He turns and walks away, then pauses. "Maisey? I love you. I'm sorry I let you down."

"Pete!" Maisey picks up a tiny stone on the beach and hurls it at him. The stone lands with a soft 'plop' on his sneaker. "I love you too."

"Message received, urban poltergeist." He picks it up.

Tucks it in his pocket before turning and resuming walking. "Message received."

"He's a good guy," I say.

"I know," Maisey says.

"Right. Not to be pesky, but it's just a beautiful time to pass to the afterlife." I point to the sun dropping over the Pacific Ocean in a big ball of glorious orange, yellow, and crimson. "It looks like Frankie's sunset painting. The one we saw at Vida V Gallery. This moment could be burned into your eternal memory. This is the perfect way for you to pass over."

She stares out, a funny look on her pretty face. "It would be nice, wouldn't it?"

"What does that mean?" I ask.

"Are you going to miss me?" Maisey asks.

"Strangely, yes." I also feel relieved. My shoulders drop from my ears and head back to where shoulders are supposed to be. I have accomplished my task as murderologist and I did so pretty quickly. "Do you have any final requests before I help you go to the Light?"

"Yes," she says.

"What?"

"Please promise that you will never ever, under any circumstances help mean, rotten Elaine if anyone murders her."

"Promise." I make the sign of the cross. "Ready?"

"Kind of." She wades into the surf. The waves lap against her dress. She smiles at me. "Love you."

My heart squeezes in my chest. "Love you back. Just do what I say, OK?"

"Maybe." She wades a little farther until she's in up to her waist.

"I, Annie Graceland, ghost whisperer and murderologist do send you, Maisey Miller to the light. You will be welcomed by the angels and—"

"See you," she says and dives under a big wave.

I shake my head. "Maisey?"

There is no Maisey.

"Maisey?"

All I see is mist rising off the ocean, sifting into the fog, shimmering, as it dances across the waves.

I blink back a few tears.

She's gone.

Epilogue

A few weeks later, I'm prepping for a March Madness catering gig I got from a movie producer who attended Mason's birthday party.

I peruse my big book of yummy desserts looking for something that basketball fans might like. Finger food. Delicious. Definitely chocolate. Maybe peanut butter? I settle on the world's best chocolate chip cookies, peanut butter squares, and brownies.

I'm in a groove, songs blasting on my playlist, cutting the brownies into squares, when my phone rings. I glance at the screen and see the call is from my Great Aunt Stella.

I pick up. "Hi, Aunt Stella. I miss you. Glad you called. What's up?"

"Annie," she says. "A bit of an odd situation. Some might call it a pickle."

"What's the pickle?"

"Remember the new ghost I told you about?"

I grab a few chocolate chips and pop them in my mouth. "Yes."

"Well, she shows up whenever she wants. She says whatever she wants."

I grab more chocolate. "That's normal, Aunt Stella. Ghosts can be like that. They tend to be demanding and irritating. It's par for the course."

"I know, but that's not why I'm calling."

"Why are you calling?"

"Well, I hate to bother you, but the ghost says she knows you. She says you were the one who told her all about the Cheesehead Lodge and how it was haunted. You told her that the Cheesehead was a lovely place to be."

My heart drops into my shoes faster than a sabotaged elevator in a skyscraper. "Did she give you a name?"

"You know my hearing's not that good anymore," she says.

"I know," I say, sweat beading on my brow. I grab more chocolate chips.

"Daisy," Aunt Stella says. "She told me her name was Daisy Diller."

"Right." My knees suddenly feel weak and I sit on the kitchen floor.

"Do you know this Daisy Diller?" she asks.

"I think I do."

"She's awfully bright. And very funny. She wants my permission to hang out here. She thinks the Cheesehead Lodge is homey. Isn't that sweet?"

"Very sweet," I say. "Must run, Auntie Stella."

"But what should I do?" she asks. "What should I tell her?"

"That's up to you," I say.

"Okay, lady, talk soon. Love you bunches."

"Love you back." I lean my head against the cabinets. The world hasn't seen the last of Maisey Miller. And for some reason?

This makes me smile.

DEAR READER: I hope you loved Annie's adventures in *Murder, Maisey, & Oopsi-Daisies*! Check out The Case of the Sugar Plum Shenanigans. It's flipping hilarious.

Description: It's Christmastime when my boyfriend, Detective Raphael announces he's traveling to Wisconsin for a job interview. Back off Dairy State. You're not getting him without a fight.

We'll stay at Great Aunt Stella's lakeside inn, the Cheesehead Lodge. *It's only a little haunted.* Besides, I'm a 'Ghost Whisperer.' I'm used to shenanigans. And, I'll only be back in Wisconsin for three days. *What could possibly go wrong?*

THE CHEESEHEAD LODGE MYSTERIES are Annie Graceland's new romantic cozy mystery series. Because things always get a little crazier in Wisconsin...

❧

BECAUSE I CAN'T STOP WRITING **these funny books** — Annie Graceland has MORE ghostly adventures in Venice Beach! Murder, Screams, & Drama Queens - Pre-order — publishes late summer / fall 2022.

DESCRIPTION: I paid a designer a decent dollop of dough to brand my bakery business.

"Annie Graceland's Killer Cupcakes" design is now plastered on everything – my website, cupcake liners, business cards. Heck, I even printed it on my flannel pajamas.

Which is why it's unfathomable that Brody Banks, an entitled social media 'influencer wannabe' decides to copy my branding.

But I wasn't the *only* person Brody copied from. He also repurposed from Valentina Valente. Valentina's a soap opera star. She's the biggest drama queen on TV.

Everyone knows you don't steal from a soap opera drama queen. It just never turns out all that well. *And Brody Banks is going to find out why...*

—

1-Click Murder, Screams, & Drama Queens - Pre-order —**now!**

❧

SIGN UP for my NEWSLETTER to get all the SCOOPS,

release info, news on sales, new books, and of course —
news about cats.

Do you love PG-13 romantic comedies? I do.

Check out Part-time Princess . Readers describe this
book as 'Ms. Congeniality meets My Fair Lady.'

**"Why can't I be a Part-Time Princess?! Amaz-
ing,** I loved this book!!" ~ London Dreaming. Turn the
page to read an excerpt.

Sign up for my NEWSLETTER to get release info,
news on sales, upcoming books, games, etc. Join my
private readers' group Pamela DuMond's Dirty Darlings
for fun. Like my Pamela DuMond Author page. Yay! Can't
wait to connect with you.

Happy reading!

Xo,

Pamela DuMond

THE CASE OF THE SUGAR PLUM SHENANIGANS

DESCRIPTION

Annie Graceland: Soon to be wed. Talks to the dead. Runs a haunted lodge called The Cheesehead.

—

It's Christmastime when my boyfriend, Detective Raphael announces he's traveling to Wisconsin for a job interview. Back off Dairy State. You're not getting him without a fight.

I'm going home with him. I'll introduce him to my weirdo family. Uncle Elliot thinks he created gum. My cousin's taking Zoom classes to become a witch.

We'll stay at Great Aunt Stella's lakeside inn, the Cheese-head Lodge.

It's only a little haunted. Secret passageways. Painted portraits that wink at you. Ghosts.

The place is booked for a Saturnalia festival. There's bound to be shenanigans. **But I'm a 'Ghost Whisperer.' I'm used to shenanigans.**

Besides, I'll only be back in Wisconsin for three days. *What could possibly go wrong?*

PRAISE

"... had me laughing out loud at Annie & her cousin Izzy's antics. " ChloeGirl

I am glad to see Anne Graceland back! I enjoyed meeting her very funny and quirky family. B. Bachus

Chapter 1

THE WISCONSIN THING

"Have I told you recently, that I lucked out in the girl-friend department?" Detective Raphael Campillio asks.

"No, actually you haven't." I stand next to the espresso maker in my itsy-bitsy dated kitchen, tamping ground beans into the filter basket. I glance at him. My boyfriend of almost three years has chocolate eyes, thick black hair, and wide muscular shoulders that this girl loves to run her hands over.

We've been getting along great, but now something feels off, I don't know why. A weird feeling brews inside me, like an irritated lady at Costco trying to yank the last rotisserie chicken from my sweaty palms. The worried voice in my head hisses that trouble's on the horizon, fish will be fried, or someone's going to be thrown into a pit of vipers, and that someone is probably me.

"Well, I have." Rafe gives me one of those looks. The one where he's going to ask me to do something I don't want to do. "You're the best girlfriend ever. Pretty. Smart. Funny."

"Cut to the chase," I say. "What do you want?"

"I want to talk to you about the Wisconsin thing." He runs a hand through his hair. "What do you think about the idea?"

"I think that it sounds like you're leaving me." I punch the button on the espresso machine, put my foot down hard on the Spanish tiled kitchen floor and try not to wince. "I'm not a fan of this idea and besides, it's my birth-day. Clearly a rotten time to bring up this kind of stuff."

"Your birthday's not for a couple of months."

"It might as well be today, because both today and my birthday are the wrong times for you to be talking about leaving me."

"For the umpteenth time, I am not leaving you. I simply want to discuss this job opportunity."

"I thought when you said you'd been offered a job in Wisconsin that you were setting me up for a bad joke." I swallow my frown. "The next thing you know, you'll be asking me when is a door not a door?"

"When it's a jar," he smiles.

"Ha-ha. Now that's a joke I can get behind." I grab a handful of homemade peanut butter cookies from the sunshine yellow jar on the counter, and set them down on a plate in front of him in my modest Venice Beach apartment. "Freshly made. Extra crunchy peanut butter. Just the way you like it."

"Thanks." He bites into one. "This isn't a joke, Annie. It's about my career and my career is important to me."

"You're right." Now I feel like a jerk. "I'm sorry. Go ahead. Tell me more." I desperately hope he won't tell me more, and yet at the same time I want him to express his feelings. Every single article I read after I Googled 'Why are boyfriends cute and irritating at the same time' said that it's good for men to express their feelings. My small, cranky voice counters that I need to stop reading lame articles like this. The espresso machine brews and hisses, sounding similar to how I feel.

"I've been wanting to take the next step in my law enforcement career path for quite a while now," Rafe says. "I've come to the sad realization that it's not happening in L.A."

"I'm sorry." I pour bitter black sludge into three demitasse cups. I toss back one for courage. "Are you sure?"

"Yes. On the other hand, the police department in Sister Bay is offering me the deputy police chief position.

I'd be in charge of community outreach, implementing programs that open conversations between law enforcement and concerned citizens, and hiring mental health response teams. I feel like I could really make a difference."

"That sounds amazing," I say with a sinking feeling, because that really does sound awesome. Rafe isn't just the hottest detective in the City of Angeles, he's also the officer with the biggest heart. This would totally be up his alley.

"Besides," he says, "there's the possibility, down the road of course, when the current chief retires, that I could be promoted to that position."

"But that might never happen. They could be enticing you with false advertising. Like those weird emails that say you've won a free five-day cruise but when you click on the link, they only want to sell you a timeshare."

"Not like that." He shakes his head. "I've talked with the chief. He didn't sound wheeler-dealer slick. He came across as earnest and well-intentioned. Like an aging Boy Scout."

"I've never trusted the Boy Scouts. Seriously, what organization has "Scout" as part of its name that doesn't sell cookies? Shifty."

"I was a Boy Scout. I was never 'shifty.'"

"Nifty," I say, grabbing a cookie. "Clean out your ears, detective." My heart thumps a bit from nerves as well as my second espresso. "Not to rain all over your 'I'm not abandoning you' parade, but won't your mother kill you if you leave L.A.?"

"My mother will visit," he says. "Just like yours does."

"What about the long-distance dating thing? It'll be a disaster."

"We're not there yet," he says. "Besides, you might enjoy visiting the Midwest more frequently than you do now."

"Do I look like the kind of sappy, weak-minded woman who picks up and moves cross country for her boyfriend?" I glare at him.

"Sappy? Never. Weak-minded. Definitely not. Overly caffeinated? Perhaps. Besides, I'm not asking you to move. I'm simply asking you to accompany me for a long weekend to check the place out."

"Oh, sure, first it's 'checking the place out.' The next thing you know we'll be at Big Dan's Sporting Goods buying matching snowmobile suits and taking selfies to post on social media."

"Humor me." He smiles.

Those dimples. That lock of black hair that falls over his forehead. The very warm, kind heart that beats in his muscular chest. Help me. "Stop," I say.

"No." He takes my hand across the table and squeezes it. "Come with me to the Heartland, Annie Graceland. The trip won't be half as much fun without you."

"You'll do fine without me." My heart plummets because I feel like he's got one foot out the door.

Theodore, my enormous, long-haired, mix-breed Himalayan cat wanders into the kitchen and meows at the top of his lungs like I haven't fed him in two months. I drop Rafe's hand. "Can't make any decisions right now. I forgot to feed my cat."

"I'll feed your cat," he says, making his way to the pantry. "Relax. You made the coffee."

"All righty." Anxiety piles up in my throat like a line of dominoes ready be pushed over. I want what's best for my boyfriend but I'm also a little selfish. I don't want him moving half way across the country -- especially not to Wisconsin.

What's wrong with Wisconsin? Nothing. I grew up there. It's great if you like lakes that are clean, and football that is down and dirty. And please don't forget the cheese. But Wisconsin represents my past and my toes are firmly planted in the sandy beaches of Venice Beach, California.

I love living in L.A. The Pacific Ocean lining our beautiful coast has miles and miles of gorgeous sun-kissed beaches. Southern California weather boasts approximately 284 sunny days a year. I have a cat. I have friends. I have a baking business that ebbs and flows. I exist slightly above the poverty level. And then there's the ghost whispering thing.

But I don't like to talk about my pinch of psychic abilities. Sure, people think talking to ghosts might be scary or exotic, but it's not. It's hard work. It's late nights and early mornings. And ghosts that just won't stop talking. The spirits of the dearly departed that find me just nag me to find their killers and move in with me until I do.

Once I manage to pass along the information to the local police department and let them do their job, I send the ghost du jour to the light. Then I spring clean my hovel, sage the place, and perform a few of my Great Aunt Stella's 'Keep Spirits Away' incantations. And yet, somehow, the spirits continue to find me, tracking me down like I'm on speed dial at the Murderology Psychic Hotline.

So, other than my cat Theodore von Pumpernickle,

the best part of my life is my boyfriend. Now he's talking about re-locating and it's making me ornery. Back off, Wisconsin. You're not getting Raphael Campillio without a fight.

"It's only for a long weekend," he says, cracking open a can of cat food. "We'll just check the place out."

"Here's the problem," I say, munching another cookie for courage or possibly just the sugar high. "If I visit Wisconsin, I'm going to have to see my family or risk excommunication, beheading, or worse."

"What's worse than beheading?" he asks, setting the dish on the floor. Theodore pounces on it, tail thwacking.

"My mother will make me sit me next to Uncle Elliot during holiday parties."

"What's wrong with your uncle? Does he, you know..." He tips a thumb to his lips.

"Meh. The whole family does that. It's more complicated. Elliot's an inventor."

"Inventors are intriguing."

"What you call intriguing, many people call crazy."

"Crazy can be fun. Did I tell you how cute you look today?" He takes my hand in his, brings it to his lips and kisses it.

"Flattery will get you nowhere," I lie.

"Flattery usually gets me everywhere," he says and waggles his eyebrows.

"Only that one time."

"I beg to differ. What has Uncle Elliot invented? Anything I know?"

"Therein lies the crazy as well as the fun part. Sometimes the inventions are real. And sometimes they're not."

"I don't understand." He takes a sip of his milk and

manages to get a milk moustache. Contrasted against the scruff on his face, he looks adorable and sexy. My fingers itch to wipe the milk away, but I refrain. "Example, please."

"Scrubby pads," I say.

"Scrubby pads?" He wipes the milk from his upper lip.

"You know, those little pads you use to scrub pots and pans."

"Right," he says. "Scrubby pads."

"Elliot says he invented them."

"Ah-ha. So that's one of the things he made up."

"No. That's one of the things he actually invented."

"Fascinating," he says reaching for another cookie. "I didn't know that."

"How could you? It's not like his name is plastered on every pad. 'Elliot's Scrubby Pads' didn't have a ring to it. That got shot down in the branding meetings."

"What else does he say he invent?".

"Gum."

"What kind of gum? Cinnamon? Spearmint? Bubble?"

"No. Just good old-fashioned 'gum.'"

Rafe frowns, looking perplexed. "But I thought — "

"He invented 'gum', along with his pal – *Mr. Wrigley*.'"

He gives me a look. "That's a little..."

"Crazy?" I twirl my finger next to my head.

"Yes. Does he have... early — "

"Nope. Mom says Elliot has been like this ever since they were kids."

"Aha."

"Do you see what we're getting into by traveling back to Wisconsin?" I ask. "We're venturing into 'crazy-pants' territory. I'm not even going to tell you about my Great Aunt Stella and her weirdo gig."

"Please Annie Graceland, best girlfriend in the world, tell me about your Great Aunt Stella and her weirdo gig." He brushes a crumb from my lips.

My heart beats a little faster because the cookie crumbs aren't the only thing he's brushing away. My resolve is disintegrating, like a pebbly cliff on a highway above the ocean.

Raphael Campillio is sweet and kind and handsome. He can't be here one day and gone the next. I can't lose him to Wisconsin. I *won't* lose him to Wisconsin. The cranky, determined girl that lives in my brain percolates on how I can shut this 'moving to the Midwest thing' down.

"Okay," I say. "Great Aunt Stella lives in Sister Bay. She owns the Cheesehead Lodge and Cabins."

"The Cheesehead? It's called that?" he asks. "Seriously?'

"Yes. Laugh all you want, but the Cheesehead's been around for sixty years. It's a little dilapidated and yet it's postcard pretty. Right on Lake Michigan, a stone's throw from downtown. A big old rambling main house, a scattering of outlying cabins, and a barn. The Cheesehead's practically an institution."

"Sounds amazing. Any cheese on the property?"

"A veritable cheese-o-rama," I say, not sure if I should tell him, yet desperately wanting to tell him that cheese is not the Cheesehead's claim to fame.

"Tell me about Great Aunt Stella."

"She's a character."

"A character in your family? I'm shocked. Tell me more."

"I hung out with her one summer in high school.

Helped her with the lodge. Painted. Fixed things. Fed the chickens. She had a pig too, if I remember correctly. It's been a while."

"That was nice of you."

"Nice of Aunt Stella, actually. Mom says I was an overly-opinionated teenager who needed to get out of the house before I became a delinquent. My folks couldn't afford summer camp, so the Cheesehead it was."

"Do anything fun that summer besides fixing things up?"

"I palled around with Aunt Stella and her BFFs. They're a bunch of tough dames. They taught me how to play poker and read tarot cards. They taught me the difference between a flathead and a Philips screwdriver, and they taught me how to bake. You have Stella to thank for these peanut butter cookies."

He stares down at the one in his hand. "She mailed these to you?"

"No, dork. The recipe. She taught me the secret recipe."

"Aha," he says. "She sounds perfectly normal. Why the eye roll?"

I am not going to spill Aunt Stella's magical beans and tell him about her séances, or that she's convinced she's been one of Sister Bay's more influential witches for the past fifty years. I go with the other thing that might make my nice Catholic boyfriend nervous. "It's not so much about Aunt Stella as it is about the Cheesehead. The lodge is haunted."

"How haunted?"

"Cute' haunted. Not icky haunted like "Poltergeist" or "Demon House.""

"Good to know." He crosses himself. "As much as I'd love to meet your aunt, I'm not sure I want to stay at the 'Demon House' Lodge when we visit Sister Bay."

"That's a terrific idea," I say. "*You* should totally stay at my great aunt's Demon House Cheesehead Lodge when *you* visit Sister Bay. Why don't we call Stella and ask her?"

"I wouldn't want to put her out," Raphael says, not meeting my eyes.

"It's not a problem. We'll catch her in the middle of cocktail hour. She'll be enjoying her obligatory glass of whatever the poison is she's tossing back these days. I'm happy to make the introduction."

"What am I going to say?"

"Just be your normal adorable self. I bet she'll even comp you a room."

"You mean comp *us* a room."

"Comp *you* a room. December holidays. I'm a baker. I've got a lot on my plate. I can't go."

"What do you have on your plate?"

"I'm catering a few parties. I promised Mort Feinberg that I'd make him two thousand Hanukkah cookies for his deli."

"Mort adores you. Maybe you could bake them a few days ahead of time. Besides, I've never stayed at a haunted lodge. The idea's starting to intrigue me."

"You'll hate it."

"I'll love it," he says. "But only if you tag along. Come on. Let's do it. It'll be fun. The city of Sister Bay will reimburse Great Aunt Stella for our room."

"You mean reimburse her for *two* rooms. She'll insist

we stay in separate rooms, as befitting an unmarried couple.”

“Two rooms it is.” He takes my hand and squeezes it. “So, it’s a yes on going back with me for the interview in Sister Bay?”

“Yes,” I say, feeling like I just got played.

“Good.” He kisses me sweetly on the lips. “I think you’re going to enjoy yourself. I think you’ll be pleasantly surprised.”

“Right,” I say, a chill zipping down my spine because he doesn’t have a clue what he’s getting himself into. “I think you’ll be surprised too.”

One-click The Case of the Sugar Plum Shenanigans.

The Case of the Sugar Plum Shenanigans. Copyright © 2021 Pamela DuMond All rights reserved.

PART-TIME PRINCESS

Royally Wed Romantic Comedy #1

☙

DESCRIPTION

Two princes are in love with Lucy. Too bad she's and imposter...

I waitress at MadDog biker bar to pay my uncle's rent at Assisted Living. I work my a** off but when I pour a pitcher of margaritas on a loser harassing my BFF -- I'm fired. I scour want-ads until I find one that doesn't make me want to hurl.

"PERSONAL ASSISTANT WANTED: Twenties.

Fab people skills. Celebrities don't intimidate you. If actress -- you can NEVER use this on your resume."

Sounds dicey as hell. I apply immediately.

Lady Lizzie Billingsley– who if you get drunk and squint could be my impeccably polished twin -- is entering into a marriage of convenience with playboy Prince Cristoph, the heir to the throne of Fredonia.

Lizzie doesn't really want a PA... she's hiring me to impersonate her, keep Cristoph's wandering eye in check while she clears up a few loose ends. Did I mention the gig pays a fortune and includes a makeover?

What could possibly go wrong?

One-click Part-time Princess now!

<u>PRAISE</u>

"Why can't I be a Part-Time Princess?! Amazing, I loved this book!!" ~ London Dreaming

"Absolutely **Freaking Hi - lar - ri - ous!!!"** ~ Avid Reader923

"AHHHHH I **LOVELOVELOVE** this Book!" ~ Maryam Dinzily

"It's **My Fair Lady meets Ms. Congeniality**..." ~ Sara Steven at Chick Lit Central Blog

One-click Part-time Princess **now!**

☙

CHAPTER 1

I sat tall, posture perfect, practically regal on a cushy, leather seat in the First Class section of British Airlines Flight #1509 to London. My Chanel traveling outfit fit me like a dream: it was casual but screamed money. *More money than I earned during the last six months at my previous job.*

I tapped my matching Chanel bag and tote with the toe of my designer shoe and slid them a few inches until they were safely tucked under the seat in front of me. Even though I was inside a plane, I still wore my new designer sunglasses: when my employer slid them on my face and instructed me to look into the mirror—they were so freaking cool! I've been called a lot of things in my life and trust me, cool wasn't one of them.

A female fight attendant leaned down toward me as passengers jostled past her on their way to the back of this fancy bus. "The flight's been delayed for a bit, Lady Billingsley. There are tornados in Oklahoma, Iowa and Kansas. We're waiting for a few passengers from connecting flights."

I glanced out the window: storm clouds bustled low in the skies overhead and a brisk wind ruffled the tarps on the baggage carts. "Bad weather," I said. "So typical this time of year in Chicago."

"Can I get you something to drink before takeoff? And, perhaps, a snack?"

I smiled and tried not to appear shocked as I looked at her nametag. "You are sweet, Kristine." The one time I'd flown before today the flight attendants practically ripped the water bottle from my sweaty hands prior to takeoff. But that was when I was in coach.

And that was when I was Lucille Marie Trabbicio—not Lady Elizabeth Billingsley.

"I'd love a..." What would Elizabeth pick if she were flying? She didn't seem to be the type to get trashed out of her mind, especially not on long trips. She wouldn't want to get dehydrated: there'd be too much damage to her skin, her make-up could smudge and possibly damage her outfit. She also wouldn't want to eat anything too salty as she might retain water. Bloating was a look that Elizabeth would not tolerate.

"A Pellegrino, please," I said. "Thank you. Is it okay—I mean might I send an urgent e-mail? It's for business."

"Of course." Kristine nodded. "Super quick! Captain says we'll be pulling back from the gate in a matter of minutes."

I nodded, reached in my purse for my state-of-the-art iPhone and flipped it open. I logged into my new Gmail account that Mr. Philips had created for my part-time job. I typed a clandestine message to his and Elizabeth's BFF, Zara, using their secret code names.

Dear Lady and The Damp:

Slight delay in departing ORD. Will check in once I've landed in London and transferred planes. Excited!! Please wish E good luck on her important mystery mission. And hang in there with the bad back thing Damp. Maybe go see a good chiropractor.

Fondly,
  Lucy

Then I remembered to use my code name, deleted *Lucy* and typed the word *Groucho*.

I fiddled with my phone until I found "Airplane Mode," and turned it on. I tucked my phone in my bag and pulled out a copy of *British Vogue*. Lady Zara encouraged me to page through the American, British and Italian versions of the fashion rag and familiarize myself with popular designers. I flipped through the magazine, glanced at the pricey clothes, expensive makeup and the pouty models. Pucci. Gucci. Valentino. Oh my!

I accepted the mineral water from the flight attendant and thanked her. I thought about my cushy signing bonus and couldn't help but smile. I'd paid my rent, as well as Uncle John's dues for the month at Vail Assisted Living. Score! I leaned back in my seat, closed my eyes and predicted that this new part-time job that I'd signed confidentiality clauses up the wazoo for would be a breeze. *I was already nailing it!*

The flight to London would take around nine hours. Plenty of time for me to review the cast of characters in Lady Elizabeth Billingsley's life, as well as their names, titles and relationships with her. I had a two-hour layover at Heathrow before my connecting flight to Elizabeth's home in Fredonia—the small, crown jewel of a country tucked in the mountains between France, Switzerland and Italy.

When someone squeezed the top of my knee. "Well, well, if it isn't Lady Elizabeth Theresa Billingsley in the flesh. Isn't *this* a sweet surprise?" A guy asked as he settled into the aisle seat next to me. My gaze fixed on his muscular hand as he caressed my knee again and then ran his index finger up my inner thigh for a very-long heartbeat.

One of the reasons I scored this part-time job was because I swore to my new employers that I could roll with the punches and improvise during unexpected events. I planned on that happening when I landed in Sauerhausen, the capital of Fredonia—not on the nine-hour flight from Chicago to London.

You've got to be kidding me. The First Class section of British Airways had perverts? I smacked him, but only managed to slap my own knee because he had lightening quick reflexes; his hand had already vanished from my thigh.

"That might leave a bruise, Princess. Which I'll happily kiss away," he said.

"Look, dickwipe," I hissed. "Who the hell do you think —" Oops. Reboot. I was now Lady Elizabeth Theresa Billingsley from post-card perfect Fredonia.

Not Lucille Trabbicio—a former cocktail waitress at MadDog bikers' bar on Chicago's Southside.

I cleared my throat and composed myself. "I apologize, sir. I do believe you accidentally bumped my knee and I over-reacted. "

"Oh, Lizzie. That was clearly no accident. 'Look, dickwipe?' Colorful language. I'm impressed. Apparently your time in the States has warmed your frosty demeanor. I can't believe my good fortune on running into you again."

He settled into his seat. "How long has it been? Fifteen months?"

I blinked. This guy not only knew Elizabeth but also had a nickname for her. I combed my brain but I didn't recognize him from any of the pictures she or Zara showed me.

Mr. Cocky pushed his leather bag under the seat in front and belted himself in. Slouched back and ran his fingers through his jet-black hair. "Did you miss me love?"

I looked at his hand that had clutched my knee just moments earlier. It was large, had no ring on the important finger and now rested on top of his thigh—which was muscular, clad in jeans and ended in slightly scuffed leather boots.

Nice. Very, very nice. Whoa—hold the door... I shook my head. No, he was *not* nice. This knee-squeezer was an opportunist and obviously depraved. My gaze traveled up and took in his finely cut sports jacket layered over a V-neck T-shirt that exposed just the right amount of black chest hair. *Hmm.*

He leaned toward me as his index finger grazed the underside of my chin. "Has anything else warmed up Lizzie?" He tilted my face upward toward his full lips. "Do you remember all the fun and games we played? All the dirty, dirty things that you and I did?" He grinned. "And then—did again. I was done at round three, but you insisted on a fourth."

Holy crap did he just say what I thought he said?

I gazed up at his face into the bluest eyes I'd seen in my entire life. The highest cheekbones. The blackest hair that was cropped in a medium-length-style with one disheveled lock that fell onto his forehead.

Hello—this might have been the best-looking man I've met in my entire twenty-one year-old life. I inhaled sharply.

And quickly realized I was being a complete dork and gave my head a shake. Get a grip, Lucy, I admonished myself. Elizabeth, Zara or Mr. Philips would have shown me this guy's picture if he were at all important. This had to be a fluke. An accident. At the worst—a chance encounter. "I think you're mistaken." I decided to hedge my bets. Elizabeth might have hired a down-on-her-luck girl, but not a dumb one. "Do we know each other?"

"There you go with that dry sense of humor I always enjoy. Breathe, Lizzie. Take-offs and landings always frighten you. Do you want me to help you through it? Just like I used to?" He held out his hand and regarded me with a twinkle in his eyes.

Kristine the flight attendant stood at the front of the plane and spoke into the intercom. "Welcome to British Air Flight 1509 from Chicago O'Hare International Airport to Heathrow, London. In a few minutes we will be pulling back from the gate. Please take a moment to review the following safety information for this plane located in the seat pocket in front of you. While our captain and co-pilots are tip-top, we'll obviously be passing through bumpy weather as we depart the Windy City."

"Um." I wondered why my tongue suddenly felt awkward inside the confines of my mouth. "Um..." Earth to Lucy. You are being paid a king's ransom. Do not screw up this job for a stunning pair of blue eyes, a little pitter-patter in your heart and a tingling in your nether-regions.

"Excuse me, sir." A short, coiffed, helmet-headed Barbara Walters type peered down her nose at us. "I'm so sorry, but I think you're in my seat. 3B?" She peered at her ticket stub. "I do believe I am in 3B."

"Oh." He pulled his ticket stub from his pants pocket and checked it. "You're right, Ma'am. I'm in 4A." He unbuckled his seatbelt. "I must have been hypnotized by this young woman's beauty."

Phew! Lucky for me I wasn't going to be stuck next to Mr. Cocky for the next nine hours.

He leaned his head toward mine and whispered, "I know you're disappointed Lizzie. I'll make it up to you, I promise. There's always the Mile-High Club. I do believe you once said those very words to me. I'll never forget my initiation. Thank you. Seriously, thank you. That was a defining moment in my life."

I coughed, clamped my hand over my mouth and collapsed forward—my boobs slapping my thighs.

He grabbed his leather duffel off the floor and stood up. "Can I help you with your bags?" he asked the woman and moved into the aisle.

"You're not only handsome, but a gentleman. Thank you for your kind offer, sir, but I'm good. My name's Jane Dawson. I could swear I've seen you before. I'm bad with names, but I never forget a face." She plopped down into the seat next to me, looked up and winked at him. "It'll come to me."

He held out his hand to her. "You can call me Nick."

Jane smiled and shook his hand. "Nice to meet you, Nick. I'll figure out how I know you. I'm good at this!" She leaned down and pushed her carry-on under the seat in front of her.

I breathed a sigh of relief and then realized I was going to be seated next to *the* Jane Dawson—the famous news reporter whose career spanned decades. I clenched my hands together and gazed out the window as the plane backed away from the terminal.

"You look familiar too, miss." Jane said. "Albeit like you've seen a ghost or recently had food poisoning. First Class on British Air is practically like opening a copy of *People Magazine*. You never know whom you'll bump into here."

I smiled at her. "It's my pleasure to meet you, Ms. Dawson. You're an amazing reporter and your career is spectacular. My name is... Elizabeth." I leaned close to her and whispered. "Thank you for saving me from that man. I'd much prefer to sit next to you during this incredibly long flight."

"Luck of the draw, Elizabeth. I was in 3B after all. Are you nervous during takeoffs dear?"

"No. I've done this a million times." The plane taxied onto the runway and I gripped the armrests like a young gold-digger holding tight to an octogenarian billionaire's arm in a Vegas wedding chapel. The aircraft paused for a few moments as thunder boomed and lightning struck in the woods and neighborhoods in the near distance.

A piece of paper shaped like a tiny airplane flew over my head and crashed onto my lap. I unfolded it and read:

My dearest Lizzie:

Liar, liar, pants on fire. Do we need to do something about that? I'm happy to help.

Always,
Nick

I scrunched the paper into a ball, flung it over my seat

back toward him and heard a low chuckle. "I'll be just fine, Ms. Dawson. Nothing out of the ordinary or unusual about today." I smiled at her, inhaled deeply and held my breath.

Except that everything about today was out of the ordinary and unusual. Because this was the biggest day of my new part-time job. And I was indeed the poster-child for Ms. Liar, Liar, Pants-on-Fire.

I closed my eyes, leaned back, tried to ignore the hot guy kicking the back of my chair and I remembered how I got here...

One-click Part-time Princess **now!**

Part-time Princess: (Royally Wed Romantic Comedy: Book 1)
Copyright © 2014 Pamela DuMond - All rights reserved.

<u>COZY MYSTERIES</u>

ANNIE GRACELAND'S CHEESEHEAD LODGE MYSTERIES - Stand Alones

The Case of the Sugar Plum Shenanigans

The Case of the Candy King's Catastrophe - COMING SOON

&

ANNIE GRACELAND COZY MYSTERIES

Stand Alones

Murder, Maisey, & Oopsie-Daisies

Murder, Screams, & Drama Queens - Pre-order

Cupcakes, Signs, & Valentines: A Novella

Cupcakes, Pies, & Hometown Guys

Cupcakes, Paws, & Bad Santa Claus

Cupcakes, Diaries, & Rotten Inquiries

Cupcakes, Sales, & Cocktails

Cupcakes, Bats, & Scaredy Cats

Cupcakes, Bars, & Rock Stars

Cupcakes, Lies, & Dead Guys

Cupcakes, Spies, & Despicable Guys

Annie Graceland Mystery Set #1: Books 1 - 4

Annie Graceland Mystery Set #2: Books 5 - 7

&

VON PUMPERNICKLE COZY MYSTERIES - Stand Alones

GOLDMITTEN: Cozy Animal Mystery #1

&

THRILLERS

21st CENTURY COURTESAN

Psychological Thriller series (Steamy)

THE PLAYER #1

THE MOVIE STAR #2

THE BELOVED #3

THE HUSBAND #4

THE DEVOTED FAN #5

21st Century Courtesan Collection: Books 1 - 2

21st Century Courtesan Complete Collection: Books 1 - 5

&

MORTAL BELOVED

Historical Fantasy Time Travel series (PG-13)

The Messenger #1

The Assassin #2

The Seeker #3

The Believer: Jack & Clara - Stand Alone

Mortal Beloved Time Travel Collection: Books 1 - 3

'SWEETER' ROMANCE

ROYALLY WED

Romantic Comedy series (PG-13)

Part-time Princess #1

Royally Wed #2

Part-time Poser #3

Royally Knocked Up #4

Royally Wed Collection: Books 1 - 4

PLAYING SWEETER

Romantic Comedy Stand Alones (PG-13)

The Story of You and Me

Ms. Match Meets a Millionaire

My Big Fake Mafia Wedding - Coming Soon

The Stupidest Holiday of the Year: A Playing Sweeter Short

Story

<u>'HOT' ROMANCE</u>

THE CROWN AFFAIR

Romantic Comedy series (Steamy)

The Prince's Playbook #1

His Majesty's Measure #2

The American Princess #3

The Duchess's Decision #4

The Crown Affair Collection: Books 1 - 4

PLAYING DIRTY

Romantic Comedy Stand Alones (Steamy)

The Client

The Matchmaker

The Bodyguard

A Playing Dirty Duet

<u>BOOKS in the WORKS</u>

Dr. Strangedove: Von Pumpernickel Cozy Animal Mystery

For more details please visit Pamela DuMond Author.

GINGER SNAPS RECIPE

GINGER SNAPS

Cookie Ingredients:

1/4 cup butter

1/4 cup molasses

1/4 cup sugar

1 1/2 cups flour

1 egg

1/4 tablespoon ginger

1/4 tsp soda

Directions:

Cream the butter in a warm bowl

Gradually beat in the sugar and molasses.

In separate bowl mix ginger, soda, and flour.

Add this mixture to the bowl with the butter, sugar and molasses.

If needed add a pinch more flour to knead this mixture.

Roll very thin on a floured baking board.
Cut Ginger Snaps with a cookie cutter and bake at 350
degrees for 6 - 8 minutes.

Let cool.

ABOUT THE AUTHOR

Stay in the loop! Sign up for Pam's Newsletter .

ABC 20/20 featured Pamela DuMond on "The Rebel: The Erin Brockovich Story."

A *USA Today* Bestselling author of *Part-time Princess* and other modern fairytales, Pam also writes cozy mysteries, romantic comedy, historical fantasy, and psychological thrillers.

Her books have been optioned for Film/TV, licensed for games, and foreign translations.

A Midwesterner at heart, Pam lives in L.A. where she consumes audio books like potato chips, practices chiropractic, and is bossed around by two opinionated cats.

Sign up for Pam's Newsletter .

Follow Pamela DuMond on Bookbub for deals.

Stalk Pamela DuMond on Instagram.

Join Pam's reader group at <u>Pamela DuMond's Dirty Darlings</u> .

For more information...
<u>www.pameladumond.com</u>

ACKNOWLEDGMENTS

Thanks Jeanie Whitemire Jackson, Cindy Sample, Heather Haven, Susan James Berger, Christine Ashworth, Kristen Warren, Maria Seager!

Thanks Amber Hamilton for bookish tasks. Special thanks to Karen Hollins at Cozy Mystery Lovers FB group.

Thanks to my readers – you rock!

Xo,
Pamela DuMond